As Pima Joe got to his feet, Clint stepped in quickly and hit the man in the face with two left jabs then danced back. As the brave stared in surprise at the blood on his fingers, Clint stepped in and hit him again . . . Although the man's nose bled more heavily, he did not take one backward step. This concerned Clint, because he felt he had hit him with a pretty decent right. The fact that the man just stood there and glared at him did not make him happy.

He braced for Pima Joe to rush again . . .

DON'T MISS THESE
ALL-ACTION WESTERN SERIES
FROM THE BERKLEY PUBLISHING GROUP

THE GUNSMITH by J. R. Roberts
  Clint Adams was a legend among lawmen, outlaws, and ladies. They called him . . . the Gunsmith.

LONGARM by Tabor Evans
  The popular long-running series about U.S. Deputy Marshal Long—his life, his loves, his fight for justice.

LONE STAR by Wesley Ellis
  The blazing adventures of Jessica Starbuck and the martial arts master, Ki. Over eight million copies in print.

SLOCUM by Jake Logan
  Today's longest-running action Western. John Slocum rides a deadly trail of hot blood and cold steel.

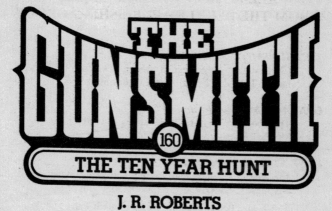

THE GUNSMITH

160

THE TEN YEAR HUNT

J. R. ROBERTS

JOVE BOOKS, NEW YORK

THE TEN YEAR HUNT

A Jove Book / published by arrangement with
the author

PRINTING HISTORY
Jove edition / April 1995

ISBN: 0-515-11593-2

A JOVE BOOK®
Jove Books are published by The Berkley Publishing Group,
200 Madison Avenue, New York, New York 10016.
JOVE and the "J" design are trademarks
belonging to Jove Publications, Inc.

PRINTED IN THE UNITED STATES OF AMERICA

10 9 8 7 6 5 4 3 2 1

THE GUNSMITH

160

THE TEN YEAR HUNT

ONE

Clint was wishing he hadn't decided to try to make town before daylight faded. It was getting pretty near that time now, and Prairie Bend, Texas, was nowhere in sight. He was short on supplies, though, and he didn't fancy camping with nothing to eat and no coffee. Coffee was the one thing he always made sure he had plenty of, and he didn't understand how he could have run out.

Suddenly, he thought he smelled some.

"Whoa, big boy," he said, reining Duke in.

Maybe it was his imagination. Maybe it was just that he hadn't had a cup all day. He could go without food longer than he could go without coffee.

He sniffed the air and there it was, plain as day. No imagining that aroma. Somebody was camped nearby and had a pot of coffee going.

1

"Okay, big fella," he said to the big, black gelding, "let's see if we can follow my nose."

By the time he located the camp it was dark. He knew he would have to be careful approaching so that he wouldn't get shot. You never rode into a man's camp without singing out first, especially not at night.

"Hello, the camp!"

There was a moment's hesitation, and then a voice called back, "Come ahead."

Clint urged Duke forward and they walked into the circle of light thrown by the camp fire.

There was one man in the camp, and he was standing, his right hand hanging close to his handgun, his left holding his rifle. Clint didn't know which gun the man would go for at the first sign of trouble, but they were both equally accessible.

"I'm out of coffee," Clint said. "In my book that's a sin."

"So?"

Clint tried again.

"I thought you might spare a cup."

The man studied him for a few moments, and Clint could see that he was also studying Duke.

"That's a handsome animal."

"Thanks," Clint said, patting Duke's neck proudly.

"Looks like he could use a rest."

"That he could."

"Step down, then," the man said. "See to your animal, and then help yourself to coffee."

"Much obliged," Clint said.

He dismounted and picketed Duke near the man's two horses, a saddle mount and a pack-horse. In unsaddling Duke he found a small rent at the bottom of his saddlebag that he hadn't seen before. It matched a hole that showed in the burlap bag he'd carried his coffee in. Without realizing he'd left a trail of coffee behind him, which explained how he had run out.

"Stupid," he said, shaking his head.

Once Duke was taken care of, Clint walked to the fire, hunkered down, and poured himself a cup. On the fire, in a black skillet, were some bacon and beans.

"Have you eaten?" the man asked.

"Not for a while."

"Run short?"

Clint nodded. "Doesn't happen often," he said, "but it happened today. Feel like a fool, to tell you the truth."

"Help yourself to some food, then," the man said.

"Thanks."

Clint took a small helping, not wanting to eat too much of the man's dinner. While he ate he studied the man and his outfit. The man was tall, rangy, well built for his age, which was over fifty, certainly. His face was the texture of leather, lined from the weather. Behind him his saddle and supplies impressed Clint. The saddle, though worn, was expensive, and the man seemed to have enough supplies for five men.

"You're outfitted well," Clint said.

"I like to avoid feeling like a fool."

"Fair enough," Clint muttered.

"Huh?"

"What's your name?"

"Randolph," the man said, "Scott Randolph."

"My name's Clint Adams."

The man stopped eating and stared across the fire.

"I've heard that name."

"I guess you have."

"Thought you'd be an older man."

"I have hopes of getting older," Clint said.

"Don't we all?"

Later Randolph made another pot of coffee, and they sat on opposite sides of the fire drinking it.

"It's good coffee," Clint said truthfully. "Strong."

"It's the only way to drink it."

"I agree."

Randolph was not a talkative man, and after a while the silence between them started to feel awkward.

"On the way to anywhere in particular?" Clint asked.

"No."

"On the way home?" Clint asked. "Or away from home?"

"Don't have a home," Randolph said. "Did, once. A ranch."

"What happened?"

"Apaches."

Clint nodded. Many settlers had lost their homes to Apaches, but not recently. Randolph must not have been talking about the recent past.

"Drove you out, huh?"

"Burned me out," Randolph said, "ran off my stock. Finished me."

"What about starting over?" Clint asked.

"Couldn't."

"Why not?"

Randolph hesitated, and Clint said, "Didn't mean to pry, Mr. Randolph."

Randolph was silent a few more moments, then said, "Most folks call me Scotty."

"Okay, Scotty. Call me Clint."

"I couldn't start over, Clint," Randolph said, "because they took my wife."

"Oh," Clint said, "I'm sorry."

"I've been lookin' for her ever since," Randolph said. "That's why I'm outfitted so well. I go months sometimes without going into a town, without seeing people. Guess that's why I kind of forgot how to talk civil."

"That's okay," Clint said. "Like I said, I didn't mean to pry, I was just trying to make conversation."

"I know," Randolph said, "but that's something I don't know how to do anymore."

"You're doing a good job."

"Thanks."

"I haven't heard of too much unrest in these parts as far as Indians attacking ranches," Clint said. "When did all this happen?"

Randolph hesitated, then said, "A while back."

Clint waited for him to add something, and when he didn't Clint shrugged and reached for the coffeepot. He poured himself a cup, and then Randolph held his out and he filled that one.

"Ten years."

"What?" Clint said, setting the pot down.

"You asked me when it happened," Randolph said. "It was ten years ago."

Clint stared at the man a few seconds and then asked, "You've been looking for your wife for ten years?"

"That's right," Randolph said, staring out into the darkness at something only he could see, "ten years."

TWO

"She was younger than me," Randolph told him. "A lot younger. Fifteen years."

"She must have loved you," Clint said.

"Yes, she did," Randolph said, "and I loved her. She was a good wife—a better one than I deserved. We worked hard on our place—too hard—she deserved better."

Clint remained silent.

"She sure didn't deserve what she got," Randolph added.

"No woman deserves that," Clint said.

"You've got that right."

"Scotty," Clint said, "if you don't mind me asking . . ."

"Go ahead."

"It's been ten years," Clint said. "What makes

you think you can find her after all this time?"

Randolph shrugged helplessly and said, "It's all I can do, Clint."

"But . . . she won't be the same woman."

"Maybe not," Randolph said, "but she's still my wife."

They sat in silence for a while before Clint asked another question.

"Where did this happen, Scotty?"

"Oklahoma."

"Why are you in Texas, then?"

"We were near the border," he said. "The braves who hit us were from Texas."

"Have you covered Texas over the past ten years?"

"I've been to Texas, New Mexico, Mexico, even Colorado and Arizona and back again. I just have to keep looking, Clint."

"But . . . for how long? When is it time to start living again?"

"Not until I find her," Randolph said miserably. "The only other thing I've thought about doin' is dyin'."

"Suicide?"

Randolph nodded.

"You can't do that."

"No," the other man said, "I can't. Not while there's still a chance I might find her."

Clint decided to stop talking about whether or not Randolph could still find her after all these years.

"What was—what's her name?"

"Helen."

"What does she look like?"

"She's small," Randolph said, "but pretty, so pretty. She's got this red hair that . . . it hangs down past her shoulders. She's . . . so pretty. . . ."

"How old was she when they took her?"

"Twenty . . . what was she? Twenty-four, or . . . or twenty-five?" Randolph was frowning with the effort to remember.

"It doesn't matt—"

"Twenty-five," Randolph said, suddenly sure. "I was forty when they took her."

Which made him fifty now, Clint figured.

They finished their coffee and Randolph said, "I'm gonna turn in."

"Yeah," Clint said, "so am I."

They each rolled themselves up in their blankets.

"Clint?"

"Yeah?"

"Come mornin' you can take whatever supplies you need," Randolph said.

"That's nice of you, Scotty," Clint said. "I just need enough to get me to the next town, Prairie Bend."

"Well," Randolph murmured, "whatever."

"Night, Scotty."

"Yeah," Randolph said, "good night."

Clint went to sleep feeling profoundly sorry for the man who had spent the past ten years in a saddle, looking for his stolen wife, hoping against hope that he'd someday happen to ride into a band of Apaches that she would be with.

That is, if she was still alive.

*   *   *

In the morning they rose at the same time, and Randolph prepared breakfast. As they ate they decided what Clint would take with him. Clint wanted only a little coffee, but Randolph insisted he take some food as well. In the end, Clint agreed, if only to stop arguing with the man.

They saddled their horses, and Clint helped Randolph pack his supplies on his other horse. As it turned out, they were heading in opposite directions.

"Every so often," Randolph said, "I head back to where it started."

"Your ranch?"

"What was my ranch, yeah."

"Where was it?"

"Near a town called January."

"January? That's an odd name for a town."

"Like Prairie Bend?" Randolph asked.

Clint had to admit that there were many towns throughout the West that had odd names. One good example was Labyrinth, Texas, where he spent a lot of time when he wasn't on the trail. In fact, he was riding through Prairie Bend on his way to Labyrinth, which was the closest thing he had to a home.

Apparently, the closest thing Scott Randolph had to a home was the town of January, where his ranch used to be.

They mounted up and shook hands.

"Thanks for the hospitality."

"Thanks for the ear," Randolph said. "It did me some good to talk about it."

"Good luck, Scotty," Clint said. "I sure hope you find her."

He watched Randolph ride off and wondered if finding his wife really would be the best thing for the man. After ten years with the Apaches, who knew who—or what—she had become?

THREE

Clint rode straight to the livery when he arrived in Prairie Bend and left Duke in the hands of the liveryman. He hadn't had to camp again since parting company with Scott Randolph, so he still had that little bit of supplies he'd borrowed from the man. He'd need to buy enough supplies to get him to Labyrinth—another two days' ride—but before he did that he was looking forward to a cold beer.

The town only had one saloon, and it was easy to find. He went up to the bar, and the bartender greeted him with a broad smile. It was nearly six p.m. and the place was almost full, which meant the man had to be busy. He wondered what the man was so happy about. It certainly couldn't have been his looks. He was very short, with thinning dark hair, a barrel chest that made him look even shorter, and he was missing a tooth in the front.

Clint made a space for himself at the bar and looked at the bartender.

"What'll you have?"

"A nice cold beer."

"Comin' up."

The man drew the beer and placed it in front of Clint, still wearing the big smile.

"Just get to town?" the man asked.

"That's right."

The bartender leaned his elbows on the bar.

"It's a nice town."

"If you say so."

"Lookin' for a place to settle?" the man went on.

"No," Clint said, "I'm looking for a place to have a nice quiet beer."

The bartender frowned for a moment, not sure he'd heard right, and finally his smile slid from his face.

"Oh, right," he said, "okay, I'll, uh, well, uh, let me know if you want somethin' else."

"Sure."

The man nodded nervously, then walked away.

"He was only tryin' to be friendly," somebody said.

Clint turned to the man standing nearest him on the left.

"What?"

"I said he was only tryin' to be friendly."

The man was tall and solidly built, with wide shoulders and a firm chin. He looked to be in his late twenties.

"Was I rude?"

"I thought so."

"Well, hell," Clint said, "I'm real sorry about that."

He was still thinking about Scott Randolph and his wife, and he wasn't feeling particularly talkative. First the bartender wanted to make conversation, and now this stranger. Now that he'd apologized, he hoped he'd be able to be alone with his thoughts.

"Maybe you should tell *him* that," the man said.

Clint wasn't sure he'd heard right.

"What?"

"His name's Nelson," the man said. "The bartender. Maybe you should apologize to him."

"Look, friend," Clint said, putting his mug down on the bar, "I'm trying to have a nice quiet drink, after which I'll leave this saloon and probably never come back. Why don't you just have your drink and let me finish mine?"

"You're real rude," the man said.

Clint stared at the man, unsure as to whether or not the man was kidding with him.

"Hey, Arch," the man said to someone else, "this fella rode into town and he's bein' rude."

"Is he, Dan?"

Clint turned and found that Arch, a big, sandy-haired man in his early thirties, was standing on the other side of him. Somehow, he guessed he had gotten between the two friends.

"Why are you bein' rude?" Arch asked.

"I don't believe this," Clint said, looking from

one to the other. "Are you two with the local church or something?"

"As a matter of fact, we are," Arch said. "We both pass the collection basket."

"Well, good for you," Clint said. With that he turned back to the bar to have his drink, even though he knew what he should have done was leave.

"We don't like strangers comin' into town and bein' rude," Dan said.

"Or startin' trouble," Arch said.

"Friends," Clint said, "I'm looking to avoid trouble."

"Then why don't you apologize to Nelson?"

"Jesus," Clint said, "get Nelson over here and I'll apologize."

He figured that would be the easiest way to handle the whole thing.

"See?" Dan said to Arch. "I told you we could get him to apologize."

"Yeah," Arch said, "you were right. He'd rather apologize than fight. He's a little yeller, don't you think?"

"I think he's a lot yeller," Dan said.

Suddenly, Clint realized that they had been playing a game with him. They weren't with the church, and they weren't concerned with him being rude, they were just looking for trouble from a stranger.

They were picking on the wrong man.

FOUR

"I get it now," Clint said.

"Do you?" Dan asked.

"He says he gets it, Dan," Arch said. "What do you think?"

"I think he should pay a fine for bein' rude in the town limits, Arch," Dan said. "What do you think?"

"I think you're right, Dan."

"What do you think, friend?" Dan asked.

Clint didn't answer.

"Hey," Dan said sharply, "I'm talkin' to you."

He spoke so loudly that the three of them were suddenly the center of attention.

"Hey, fellas," the bartender said in a tone that was not very forceful, "not in here, huh?"

"Butt out, Nelson," Dan said.

Well, at least the bartender's name really was Nelson.

"We got business with this man," Arch said. And then to his crony, he added, "He's ignorin' you, Dan."

"Yeah, he is. Hey, friend, are you ignorin' me?"

Clint looked at him and said, "That's what I'm doing . . . friend."

"That ain't gonna keep you from payin' the fine, you know."

"I'm not paying any fine," Clint said. "I'd advise you and your friend to go and look for another candidate."

"Another one?" Dan asked. "Hell, ain't no other stranger came into town today. Was there another stranger in town today, Arch?"

"Not today, Dan."

"See?" the man said. "There ain't nobody else."

Clint looked away and said, "Then wait for somebody else."

"I don't think so," Dan said. He reached over and poked Clint's arm. "I think you're it."

"I don't think so."

When Dan reached out to poke Clint again, he was ready. As the man's fingers dug into his arm, he flipped the contents of his beer mug—which was half full—into the man's face.

He kept turning to his right until he had turned completely around. Arch was coming toward him, and Clint swung the beer mug and caught the onrushing man on the jaw. As Arch went down, Clint continued to turn until he was facing

Dan again, who was wiping beer from his face.

"Why you—" he said, and he went for his gun. Before he could reach it, though, Clint had his gun pressed underneath Dan's chin, and the man stopped cold, his eyes widening.

"Hey—" he said.

Clint reached out and plucked Dan's gun from his gun belt.

"Nelson?"

"Yessir?"

"Put this behind the bar for me, will you, please?" Clint asked.

"S-sure."

Nelson took the gun and placed it underneath the bar.

"Somebody want to get that other fella's gun and hand it to Nelson?"

For a moment nobody moved, but then someone leaned over, took Arch's gun from his holster, and handed it to Nelson.

"Okay," Clint said to Dan, "you and me are going to the sheriff's office."

"We was just havin' some fun, mister," Dan said.

"Fun time's over, friend," Clint said. "Let's go."

"What about him?" Dan asked, pointing at Arch, who was still out cold on the floor, his chin swollen to double its normal size.

"I think he'll be there long enough for the sheriff to come and get him. Move!"

Dan started for the door, with Clint behind him, but before Clint left he said to the bartender, "Nelson?"

"Yessir?"

"If I was rude to you, I'm sorry."

Nelson swallowed hard and said, "Think nothin' of it."

FIVE

Clint marched Dan over to the sheriff's office, and they entered without knocking. Clint pushed the man into the office ahead of him, whereupon Dan stumbled and fell. The sheriff jumped up from behind his desk and stared at Dan as the man got back up.

"Dan," he said, "what the hell are you doin' here?"

"It ain't my fault, Sheriff," Dan said, dusting himself off. "This stranger pulled a gun on me an' Arch—"

"He pulled a gun on you two?"

"That's right."

"For no reason?"

"That's right."

"Yeah," the sheriff said, "right."

"Look, Sheriff—" Dan started.

"Shut up, Dan!" the sheriff snapped, looking at the man with distaste. He looked at Clint, his expression changing very little, and asked, "Who are you?"

"My name's Clint Adams, Sheriff."

"Adams," the lawman said. "Sure, I've heard of you. Just get into town?"

"Not even an hour ago."

"And already you had trouble with this fool and his cousin?"

"You know them?"

"I know them real well," the sheriff said. "My name's Pyle, by the way. Tell me, did they try that story about paying a fine for bein' rude?"

"That's the one."

"How insistent did they get?"

"They got pushy," Clint said, "and I threw my beer in this one's face."

The sheriff closed his eyes, as if he were in pain.

"Don't tell me he went for his gun?"

"He did."

"And he's still alive?"

"Despite what you may have heard, Sheriff," Clint said, "I keep my killings to a minimum."

"You, uh, didn't kill Arch, did you?" the sheriff asked.

"No," Clint said, "but he's on the floor of the saloon, unconscious. You might want to send someone over there to pick him up."

"I'll have my deputy go over," Pyle said. He was a big man with a bushy beard and small, twinkling eyes that belonged on a ten-year-old boy rather than a lawman. "Do you want to press charges against these two fools?"

Clint sighed and holstered his gun.

"Would it do any good?"

"They'd get fined."

"And I'd have to stay and wait for a judge?"

"I'm afraid so."

"How about you keep them in jail overnight?"

"Hey, you can't do that!" Dan said. "We got to—"

"Shut up, Dan!" Pyle said. He looked at Clint and said, "I can do that."

"Good," Clint said, "then I'll leave him in your care."

"How long do you plan to stay in town, Adams?" Pyle asked.

"Well, if I'm guaranteed no trouble from these two again, overnight. I'll be leaving in the morning."

"You won't have any trouble from them," Pyle said. "I promise you."

"Okay, Sheriff," Clint said. "Thanks."

"Hey," Dan said, "I want him arrested."

"For what?" Pyle asked.

"For . . . for . . . for throwing beer in my face!"

"I'm afraid that ain't against the law, Dan," Pyle said. He picked up his keys and said, "Come on, there's a cell waiting for you."

"Damn!" Dan said. "No more fun tonight."

As Clint was going out the door, he heard Pyle say, "You got that right."

SIX

After Clint left the sheriff's office he had to go back to the saloon to get his saddlebags. When he arrived, Arch was being helped from the place by a couple of men.

"The sheriff is sending someone over for him," Clint told the men.

They, in turn, dropped Arch into a chair outside the saloon, then turned and went back in. Clint followed them and looked around for his saddlebags, which had been at his feet.

"Are you lookin' for these?" Nelson, the bartender, asked. He was holding the saddlebags up behind the bar.

"Yes," Clint said, walking over to the bar and taking them, "thanks."

"Mister?"

"Yeah?"

"What do I do with Dan's and Arch's guns?"

"Save them for the sheriff, or his deputy," Clint said. "One of them'll be by for them."

"Uh, do you want a beer?" Nelson asked. Then he added, "On the house?"

"No, thanks."

"Come back anytime, then," Nelson said. "It'll be waitin' for you."

"Sure."

Clint left the saloon and walked to the Prairie Bend Hotel. He got himself a room and arranged for a bath.

"Just come down whenever you're ready, sir," the clerk said. He was a fussy little man in his forties who fluttered his hands around when he spoke. It was distracting. "I'll have someone draw the bath for you."

"Have it done now," Clint said, "and I'll be right down."

"Okay," the clerk said. "Hot or cold?"

Clint watched the man's hands wave around, then looked away.

"Hot."

"Just come down when you're ready, then."

"Thanks."

He went up to his room to stow his gear, then took a clean shirt downstairs with him. The clerk showed him to a room in the back, where a tub of hot water was waiting for him. The tub was enclosed by wooden walls, making him feel like he was in a box. While he was bathing, two other men came in and went into two other wooden boxes to take baths. Clint was lying with his head back, letting the hot water soothe his muscles, when he suddenly became aware of a conversation between the two men.

" . . . damnedest thing, I gotta tell you," one man said. "There was these Apaches, see, a dozen of 'em."

"A dozen?" the other man asked skeptically.

"That's right."

"Twelve?"

"Yeah, twelve," the first man said. "You gonna let me tell this story?"

"Okay, go ahead."

"There I was, up on this hill, and I stop my horse because in another minute I was gonna ride right up on them."

"Was they friendly?"

"How do I know, was they friendly?" the first man said. "I didn't go down and ask 'em."

"What'd you do?"

"I turned my horse around and went back down the hill, and then I rode around those murderin' redskins."

"What're ya callin' 'em murderin' redskins for?" the second man asked. "You said you didn't check to see if they was friendly or not."

"Every redskin has killed a white man sometime," the first man said, as if explaining a school lesson to a small child. "That makes 'em all murderers."

"I'm glad you explained that to me," the second man said.

"Are you gonna let me finish this story?"

"I thought you was finished," the second man said.

"Not yet."

"Why not? You rode around them, didn't you?"

"Yeah, I did," the man said, "but not before I saw somethin' funny."

"Like what?"

"Like a white woman."

Clint sat up straighter in the tub.

"A white woman? With a dozen Indians?"

"That's right."

"Was they rapin' her?"

"Nope."

"Killin' her?"

"Nope."

"Then what?"

"Nothin'."

"What do ya mean, nothin'?"

"I mean nothin', like I said," the first man said. "They wasn't doin' nothin' to her."

"They musta been doin' somethin' to her."

"If you'd let me finish the story, I'll tell you what she was doin'."

"Okay, go ahead, finish."

There was a moment of silence, and Clint almost called out to the man.

"She was cookin'."

"What?"

"Like I said," the first man said, "she was cookin' for them."

"A white woman cookin' for redskins?"

"That's right."

"Then she musta belonged to one of them," the second man said. "You know, like a white squaw or somethin'?"

"I guess so," the first man said.

"Wait a minute."

"What?"

Clint heard some movement as the water sloshed in the other tubs, and he listened intently, so as not to miss any words.

"Are you sure she was a white woman?"

"Sure I'm sure."

"Was she dressed like a white woman?"

"Well, o' course she wasn't dressed like a white woman," the first man said. "She was dressed like a squaw."

"Then how do you know she was a white woman?"

The first man snorted and said, "That was easy."

"What made it so easy?"

The first man paused for dramatic effect and then said, "She had red hair!"

SEVEN

"You don't . . ." the second man was saying, but his voice faded out. Clint suddenly realized that both men had left the room, their baths finished.

"Jesus," he said, and hurriedly got out of the tub. Could they have been talking about Scott Randolph's wife? How many red-haired white women could there be living among Apaches?

He dried himself off somewhat and dressed quickly. His back was still wet, and his shirt stuck to him as he strapped on his gun and ran out into the hall, barefoot with his boots under one arm. He looked up and down the hall, but there was no one in sight.

He ran out to the hotel lobby, where he startled a man and a woman, who stared at his bare feet. He hurried to the desk and said to the clerk with the fluttering hands, "Hey, you."

The man turned around and asked, "Was your bath satis—"

"What happened to the two men who were back there with me?"

The clerk frowned.

"What two men?"

"There were two other men back there with me taking baths," Clint said. "They left before me. What happened to them?"

"I'm sorry," the clerk said, "I didn't see—"

"You must have seen them," Clint said. "They just came out of the room."

"Sir," the clerk said, "they could have walked the other way and gone up the back steps."

"There are back steps?"

"Yes," the man said. "They lead to the second floor, where the rooms are."

"Well, didn't they have to go in this way, past you?" Clint asked.

"They would have, if they had arranged for their baths with me, but you are the only guest I arranged a bath for," the clerk explained.

"How could they have taken baths without arranging it with you?"

"That's easy," the man said. "You were my first guest for the day. I just came to work. They must have arranged their baths with Eldon."

"Who's Eldon?"

"The clerk who was working before me, of course."

"But they came into the room after I did?"

"Perhaps they didn't come down as fast as you did for your bath after arranging for it?"

Clint thought back and thought he might have heard one of the men comment on how the water wasn't so hot anymore.

"Damn it," he said.

"What?"

"Never mind," Clint said. "Look, where can I find Eldon?"

"I supposed he went home—"

"Where does he live?"

"Look here," the clerk said, frowning, "I can't tell you that—"

Clint took out a gold eagle and showed it to the man, whose hands stopped fluttering when his eyes fell on the coin.

"Where does he live?" Clint asked.

The clerk told him where Eldon lived, and even gave him directions on how to find it. Clint gave him the money.

"If there's anything else I can do for you . . ." the clerk was saying, but Clint didn't hear the rest because he was already out the front door.

EIGHT

Clint followed the directions given him by the desk clerk and came to the hardware store. The other clerk, Eldon, was supposed to live in rooms above the hardware store. The clerk had also told him that there was a stairway in the alley next to the store. Clint went into the alley and saw the stairway, which led up to a second-floor door. He went up the stairs and knocked.

"What?"

"Is your name Eldon?"

There was no answer at first, and then the voice called out, "Who wants to know?"

"I'm a guest at the hotel."

"I'm off duty."

"I want to ask you a question."

"About what?"

"Can you open the door?"

"Look," the voice said, "I'm off duty—"

"I'll pay you."

There was a moment's pause, and then the door opened. The man was tall and lanky, dark-haired, probably in his twenties. He had skin the color of white soap.

"How much?"

"A dollar."

The man's hair was disheveled, and he appeared like he'd been lying in bed.

"You woke me up for a dollar?"

Clint doubted the man had fallen asleep yet, but he played along.

"I tell you what," he said, "my question is about two men. I'll give you a dollar a man."

Eldon thought it over, then got a crafty look in his eyes.

"What's the question?"

"It's simple," Clint said. "Who were the last two men who asked you for baths?"

Eldon waited a few seconds more and then frowned at Clint and asked, "That's it?"

"That's it."

"Where's the money?"

Clint took out two silver dollars. He gave Eldon one, and held on to the other one.

"The names."

"Mr. Holbrook in room six . . ." Eldon said, and then stopped.

Clint handed him the other dollar.

" . . . and Mr. Tanner in room eight."

"Thanks, Eldon," Clint said.

"Sure," Eldon said, "anytime."

"You can go back to sleep now."

"To tell you the truth," Eldon said, "I wasn't asleep yet."

Clint went down the steps and said to himself, "Big surprise."

From upstairs Eldon called, "Do you want to know what they look like?"

Clint stopped, turned, and looked up the steps.

"How much extra will that cost?"

Eldon smiled and said, "I'll throw that in."

He returned to the hotel and went right to the second floor. He went first to room six and knocked. When there was no answer, he tried room eight. When there was no answer to his knock there, he cursed and went back down to the lobby.

"What's your name?" he asked the fussy clerk.

The man turned and frowned.

"Keith."

"Keith, do me a favor."

"If I can."

"Put your hands on the desk."

Keith hesitated, then said, "What?"

"Put your hands on the desk."

"Why?"

"Just put them there."

Keith still hesitated.

Clint sighed and said, "I'll give you a dollar if you'll put them on the desk."

Keith thought it over, then carefully placed his hands on the desk, palms down.

"Why?" he asked.

"Because your hands fly around when you talk and it's very distracting."

"They do?"

"Yes, they do," Clint said. "I'm looking for the man in room six and the man in room eight. Uh, Holbrook and Tanner."

Keith turned and looked into the boxes behind him without taking his hands off the desk.

"They're not in their rooms."

"I know they're not in their rooms," Clint said. "When did they go out?"

"A couple of minutes ago, I guess."

"Do you know where they went?"

"No, sir."

"You didn't hear them talking?"

Keith thought a moment.

"Yes, I think I did."

"What were they saying?"

The clerk thought another moment before answering.

"I believe one of them wanted to eat here in the hotel, and the other said the food was . . . uh, bad." Keith looked around to see if anyone had heard him say something so disloyal.

"Go on," Clint said, "no one heard you. What did they say then?"

"Nothing," Keith said, "they just left."

"So they were going to look for someplace else to eat."

Keith looked surprised.

"I suppose so."

"Where's a likely place to eat?"

"Well, there's a couple of cafés . . ." Keith said, and proceeded to give Clint directions to them.

"Thanks."

Clint turned to leave, and Keith said, "Hey, where's my dollar?"

"Look under your hand," Clint said, as he went out the door.

Keith frowned down at his hands, then removed first the right one, and then the left. Sure enough there was a silver dollar underneath his left hand.

"How—" he started to ask before realizing that Clint was gone.

NINE

Clint found two men fitting the descriptions given him by Eldon in the second café Keith had sent him to. They were a hard pair to miss. One man—Holbrook, according to Eldon—was heavyset and squat, while the other—Tanner—was tall and slightly stooped. These two men were seated, but they fit the descriptions nevertheless. Tanner even stooped while seated, so that he looked as if he were hovering over his plate.

"Can I help you, sir?" a waiter asked Clint.

Suddenly, Clint realized how hungry he was, and he asked the waiter for a table.

"Just follow me," the man said.

He led Clint to a table against the left wall, virtually across from where the two men were eating. Clint ordered the first thing that came to mind, a steak and some vegetables, and a pot of coffee.

He noticed that the two men were talking and eating slowly. He decided to wait until they had finished eating before he approached them. Meanwhile, he'd eat his own meal.

Clint was almost finished with his food when he noticed that the two had completed their meals. He waved the waiter over before they could.

"Would you bring me those gentlemen's check and tell them that their meal is on me?"

"Yes, sir," the waiter said, and handed Clint their check.

Clint watched as the waiter walked over to the table and exchanged a few words with the men. They looked over at Clint and frowned. Then the waiter left and the two men talked together before standing up and approaching Clint's table.

"Are you payin' for our food?" the shorter man, Holbrook, asked. At least, Clint hoped it was Holbrook.

"If your names are Holbrook and Tanner, I am."

The two men exchanged a glance.

"What if that ain't our names?" the taller man asked.

Clint laughed.

"Well, I guess that means I'm stuck with your check, doesn't it?"

The two men exchanged another glance, this one puzzled.

"*Are* you Holbrook and Tanner?"

"We are," Tanner said, "but we don't know you, stranger."

"No," Clint said, "no, you don't."

"But you know us?" Holbrook asked.

"Well, not really," Clint said. "I mean, I was taking a bath when you were, and I heard a conversation that you had. I tracked you down from there."

"Is that so?" Holbrook asked.

"That's right."

"Why?" Tanner asked.

"Why were you listenin' to our conversation?" Holbrook asked.

"Well, it was kind of hard not to," Clint reminded them. "You fellas were talking pretty loud."

"So what's your interest in what we were talking about?" Holbrook asked.

From the sound of their voices, it was Tanner who had been telling Holbrook about the red-haired woman and the Apaches.

Clint addressed himself to Tanner.

"I'm interested in the red-haired woman you were talking about," he said.

Tanner frowned.

"You lose a red-haired woman to Apaches?"

"A friend of mine did," Clint said.

"You think this might be the one?" Tanner asked.

"I don't know," Clint said, "but I'd sure like to find out. To do that I'd have to know where you saw the Apaches."

The two men were silent.

"Are you willing to tell me?" Clint asked.

Tanner looked at him and said, "If you throw in two more cups of coffee, we are."

"Have a seat," Clint said, and signaled the waiter for two more cups.

When Tanner and Holbrook had their coffee, Clint asked, "Where did you see the Apaches?"

"Well," Tanner said, frowning, "I'm not rightly sure—I mean, about the exact spot."

Disappointed, Clint asked, "Can you give me some idea of the town you were near?"

"I think the first town I came to was a place called Faith Hill."

"Faith Hill?" Clint asked. He had never heard of it.

"Uh-huh," Tanner said. "It's about two days' ride north of here."

"And where did you see the Apaches?"

"I think it was about a day and a half's ride west of that," Tanner said.

"You can't pin it down any better than that?" Clint asked.

Tanner looked sheepish.

"Look, mister, I don't travel by horseback very much. I was on a business trip. I got a business in Little Fork, which is a couple of days' ride from here. I just stopped for some sleep and a bath. Once I get back there I don't think I'll get on a horse for a long time to come."

"I see."

"My sense of direction ain't so good," the man continued, "and my memory is even worse."

"You said something about a hill."

"Did I?"

"When you were bathing," Clint said. "You said something about coming to the top of a hill and seeing the Indians with the woman."

"That's what you said, Lyle," Holbrook said to Tanner. "It surely is."

"Then that's probably what happened," Tanner said. "Let me think a minute."

Clint had finished his meal and pushed his plate away.

"Might you think better over a drink at the saloon, Mr. Tanner?"

Tanner's face brightened and he said, "You know, I might."

"Then why don't we go over there and talk?" Clint asked. He looked at Holbrook and said, "You come, too, Mr. Holbrook."

"Don't mind if I do."

Clint figured Holbrook might be able to say something that would jog the other man's memory.

They stood up, Clint paid the checks, and the three of them left and walked to the saloon.

TEN

"Back for that free drink?" the bartender, Nelson, asked Clint.

"I'll pay for my drink," Clint said. "I'll need three beers."

"Comin' up," Nelson said with a shrug. Couldn't force a man to take a free beer.

Upon entering the saloon Clint had instructed Holbrook and Tanner to get a table while he got the drinks. He turned with the three beers in hand and found, with some satisfaction, that the men had managed to secure a table at the back of the room. He negotiated himself across the crowded room with a minimum of spillage and set the three beers down on the table.

"Have you managed to remember anything else, Mr. Tanner?" he asked.

Tanner held up a finger, asking Clint to wait a moment, and then drained half of the beer in his mug.

"I did think of something," he said then.

"What?" Clint asked.

"A tree."

"A tree?" Holbrook asked. "You didn't say anything to me about a tree."

"I just remembered it," Tanner said.

"What kind of a tree?" Clint asked.

"That's just it," Tanner said, "I don't know about trees. I don't know what kind of tree it was."

"Then what made you remember this tree?" Clint asked.

"The shape of it," he said. "It was on the top of the hill when I was looking down at the Apache camp."

"What was so odd about the shape?" Holbrook asked.

"Well, it was . . . round. I mean, it looked round . . . I mean, it looked like a circle on a trunk."

Clint tried to follow the man's words and then got an idea.

"Wait here." He got up and walked to the bar.

"Another?" Nelson asked.

"Nelson, I need a scrap of paper and a pencil."

"Paper and pencil?"

"That's right."

Nelson frowned, then brightened.

"Wait."

He went off to the other end of the bar, then came back with some brown paper that might

have come from a general store and a short stub
of pencil.

"Will this do?"

"That'll do fine," Clint said. "Thanks."

He took the pencil and paper back to the table
and sat down.

"Can you draw me a picture of the tree?"
he asked Tanner, pushing the paper and pencil
toward him.

Tanner paused a moment, then nodded and
said, "I think I can."

Clint and Holbrook worked on their beers slowly while Tanner struggled to draw a picture of
the tree he was thinking about. Several times he
stopped and closed his eyes, as if trying to conjure
up an image of the tree. Finally he completed
the picture and pushed the piece of paper over
to Clint.

"There!" he said.

Clint turned the paper around and looked at it.
The picture seemed to be of a gnarled tree with a
thick trunk, and above the trunk the tree somehow managed to describe an almost perfect circle.

"There were no leaves on this tree?" Clint
asked. "It was as bare as you have it drawn here?"

"That's right."

"Was it alive or dead?"

Tanner thought a moment.

"I guess it would have had leaves if it was alive,
huh? So it must have been dead."

A dead tree, Clint thought, that looked like a
circle on a trunk, a day and a half's ride west of
a town that was a full two days' ride from here.

Perfect.

ELEVEN

Holbrook and Tanner left Clint in the saloon, where he had another beer and thought the situation over. Of course, the red-haired woman Tanner had seen with the Apaches did not have to be Scott Randolph's wife, but did he have the right not to try and get Randolph this information? After all, the man had confided in him, had practically opened his heart to him. This was too much of a coincidence—especially for a man like Clint who didn't believe in such things.

He decided that the best thing he could do was send a telegram to January, Oklahoma, so that it would be there waiting for Randolph when he got there. He'd simply explain what it was he had found out and let the man take it from there himself.

He left his table and walked over to the bar.

44

"Another?" Nelson asked.

"No, thanks," Clint said. "Can you tell me where the telegraph office is?"

"I can," Nelson said, "but at this time of the evening they'd be closed."

"That's okay," Clint said. "I'll go by in the morning."

"Okay . . ." Nelson said, and proceeded to give him directions.

"Much obliged," Clint said, and left the saloon.

Since the telegraph office would be closed, he decided to go back to his hotel instead. He felt tired, hoping that it was simply from the day's events, and not from the fact that he was getting older.

On the way to the hotel he realized how much trouble he was going to have trying to describe the landmark tree in a telegraph message to Scott Randolph. And without that how was the man going to find the spot?

Jesus, he thought, he was probably going to have to go to Faith Hill and maybe meet Randolph there. Together, they could go looking for the tree, and the band of Apaches, and the red-haired woman, who he hoped would turn out to be Randolph's wife.

The man had a right to find his wife, didn't he? Even after ten years? Even if when he found her she wouldn't want to go with him?

Clint couldn't imagine what it must be like for Randolph, not knowing all these years if his wife was alive or dead. It must have been hell. He hadn't spent much time in the man's company, but he had come away liking him and wishing him well. Now maybe he had a chance to help him, and he couldn't pass that up, could he?

In the morning he'd send a telegram to January, telling Scott Randolph to meet him in the town of Faith Hill, Texas. Tanner had explained that he thought that the spot with the tree was a day and a half's ride west of Faith Hill, which would put them in the panhandle. Randolph would be approaching the town from the north, so they wouldn't be retracing ground he would have already covered.

Clint approached the hotel and was about to enter when he heard a sound to his left, perhaps a foot scraping the wooden boardwalk. He turned just in time to avoid being struck on the head by a club. Clint raised his left arm and took the blow on the forearm. He felt the pain to his shoulder and then the arm went numb. Still, he was able to close his hand around the club and avoid being struck again. Suddenly, he became aware that there was more than one man attacking him. He was at a gross disadvantage in the dark, so he did the only thing he could. He drew his gun and fired at the man who was still holding the club. He heard the man grunt in pain as the bullet penetrated his flesh, and suddenly the grip on the other end of the club disappeared. After that he heard urgent voices.

"Oh, hell, he shot Dan," someone said. "Let's get out of here."

He thought he could make out the silhouettes of two men running away. The third man had slumped to the boardwalk. Clint discarded the club in his left hand and holstered his gun, then leaned over the man to examine him.

Even in the dark he could tell he was dead.

Someone came out of the hotel. Clint looked up and saw that it was Keith, the desk clerk.

"What happened?"

"Go get the sheriff," Clint said. "I just killed a man."

TWELVE

"You were supposed to keep him in jail, Sheriff," Clint said.

"I know."

"What happened?"

Pyle shook his head. He was sitting behind his desk, with Clint standing across from him. It was barely an hour since Clint had been attacked. It was only after they had removed the body to the undertaker's office that Clint realized that the man who attacked him was Dan, one of the men from the saloon.

"He swore he wouldn't go after you, Adams," the lawman said.

"Well, you can see how he meant that, can't you?" Clint asked. "Now because you let him out I had to kill him."

"Why don't you tell me again what happened—"

"I've told you enough times already, Sheriff," Clint said, cutting the man off angrily. "He came at me with an axe handle."

"And you shot him."

"That's right."

"Couldn't you have stopped him some other way?"

"Like how?" Clint asked. "Let him break the axe handle over my head?"

"Well, there might have been some other way than shooting him."

"Sheriff," Clint said, "it was dark, and I had no idea if he was going to go for a gun or not. I also had no idea how many men he had with him. I did what I thought I had to do to protect myself."

"Well . . ."

"Is there something wrong with that?"

"Well, I don't think that's for me to say—"

"Look, I won't be bothering you and your town anymore," Clint said. "I plan on leaving come morning."

"Oh . . ."

"Oh, what?"

"I, uh, don't think I can let you leave, Adams," the sheriff said, though not forcefully.

"What?"

"It's just that . . . well, you did kill a man, you know, and we really should wait for a judge—"

"Are you telling me I can't leave town?"

Sheriff Pyle stared at Clint, and then looked away quickly.

"Well, I'm not telling you—"

"Are you asking me to stay until you can get a judge here?"

"I guess I am—"

"Well, I'm not staying," Clint said. "You find the men who were with him and they'll tell you what happened."

"What if they lie—"

"They won't," Clint said. "They hightailed it when the going got tough. I don't think they're going to be able to lie to you."

"I still should—"

"What you should have done, Sheriff," Clint said sharply, "was keep that man in jail like you said you would. If you had done that, he wouldn't be dead."

"I know that."

"Where's the other one?" Clint asked. "Arch? Did you let him out, too?"

Pyle looked away.

"Well, I guess I won't be getting any sleep tonight," Clint said bitterly.

"Sorry—"

"What the hell were you thinking?"

Pyle looked at Clint and said, "I couldn't help it, Adams."

"Why not?"

"Dan and Arch," he said, "they're cousins."

"I know they're cousins," Clint said. "You told me that when we first talked."

"No, you don't understand," Pyle said. "I mean they're my cousins, too."

"Your cousins."

"That's right."

Clint hesitated a moment, and then decided to stay mad instead of giving in.

"And you want to wait for a judge to come to town so you can tell him that you let two prisoners out of jail because they're your cousins?"

"Uh . . . " Pyle said, uncertainly.

"What do you think would happen if that got out, Sheriff?" Clint asked. "How long do you think you would hold on to your job then?"

"Uh . . ."

"You didn't think of that when you let them out, did you?"

"No," Pyle said honestly, "I didn't."

Clint stared at the man for a moment, then decided he'd had enough of him.

"Look, Sheriff," he said, "can you find your cousin Arch and make sure he doesn't try to kill me tonight?"

"I don't think he will," Pyle said. "He only did what Dan told him to do."

Clint glared at the lawman.

"All right," Pyle said, "I'll find him and tell him."

"Make him listen," Clint said, moving toward the door. "I don't want to have to kill anyone else tonight."

THIRTEEN

Clint didn't exactly trust the sheriff to control his other cousin, Arch, so he took some precautions before turning in for the night. He jammed a chair beneath the doorknob and took the pitcher from the dresser and set it on the windowsill, so that anyone trying to sneak in would knock it over. After that he went to bed, but slept with one eye open.

He woke in the morning with a start and quickly looked at the window and the door. Both were still secure. From the amount of light coming in the window he figured it wasn't much after first light. He doubted the telegraph office would be open this early, but maybe he'd be able to get breakfast in the hotel dining room and collect Duke from the livery before he sent the telegram to January, Oklahoma.

Clint got dressed, but left his gear in his room. He decided he'd have breakfast before he checked out.

He went downstairs and found the dining room open, although he was the only diner at the time. He ordered breakfast—steak and eggs, since he was going to be on the trail again—and started on a pot of coffee while he waited. Over the coffee he realized he was going to have to buy some supplies, and he hoped the general store would open early enough for him to do that. If it wasn't open by the time he left, he figured he'd try to make it to the next town. He wanted to try to make good time to Faith Hill, even though he knew that arriving there quickly might mean having to wait for Scott Randolph to arrive. Still, once he was there he might be able to find out something about Apaches in the area.

Just as his breakfast came, he saw Sheriff Pyle out in the lobby. It took a moment, but after the clerk told the sheriff where Clint was, Pyle entered the dining room.

"I don't want to interrupt your breakfast," the man said apologetically.

"What can I do for you, Sheriff?"

"Well . . . you did say you was leavin' today . . . I just—"

"Just wanted to check and make sure?"

"Well . . ." Pyle said sheepishly.

"Don't worry, Sheriff," Clint said. "I'm leaving. You could help me with something, though."

"What's that?"

"What time does the general store open?"

"I believe at eight a.m.," Pyle said. "You'll be needin' supplies for your trip?"

"That's right."

"I could check for you—"

"That's okay," Clint said. "I've still got to collect my horse from the livery. I should be over there by eight, though."

"Well, all right," Pyle said. "Uh, you, uh, have yourself a safe ride now, you hear?"

"Sure," Clint said, wondering what the man was so nervous about. "Tell me something else, will you?"

"Uh, sure . . . if I can."

"Did you ever find your other cousin?"

"Arch?"

"That's the one."

"Uh, no, I never did. Uh, you didn't have any trouble with him, did you?"

"No," Clint said, "no trouble."

"Good, good," the sheriff said.

"Have a good morning, Sheriff."

"Uh, thanks, you, too. . . ."

Clint watched the man walk out, his gait very uncertain, as if he wanted to look behind him but didn't dare. Something was on the sheriff's mind, something he wasn't quite ready to own up to.

Clint decided not to give it any thought until he was finished with his breakfast.

FOURTEEN

By the time Clint finished his leisurely breakfast, his mind had reasoned things out. He ordered another pot of coffee, even though he didn't really want one. When men were waiting to ambush you, it was better to make them wait, make them get impatient and sweat.

He was sure that not only was cousin Arch waiting at the livery to ambush him, but the other cousin—Sheriff Pyle—as well. And who knew how many more cousins there were?

There was no way he could avoid the confrontation that was waiting for him at the stable. He had to go and reclaim Duke. There was no way he could leave town without the big gelding—and even if there were a way, he wouldn't take it. As much as he preferred to avoid trouble, there was no way he was going to run from it.

It was obvious to him that in order to stay alive he was going to have to do some killing this morning. The awkward part of that was going to be if he had to kill the sheriff. True, the man wasn't much of a sheriff, but he was still the local law.

Clint finished the second pot of coffee and paid his bill. He went up to his room, collected his gear, and went downstairs to check out.

"Will you do me a favor?" he asked the clerk, Eldon.

"Sure."

"Hold my gear for me?"

"How long?"

Clint handed over his saddlebags.

"Oh, a half an hour or so, I guess."

Eldon put the saddlebags down at his feet and said, "Yeah, sure, why not?"

Clint turned to leave, then stopped and turned back.

"One more thing."

"What?"

"If I don't come back," Clint said, "the saddlebags are yours."

Eldon's eyes widened, as he understood the implications of the statement.

"Well . . . thanks."

"And another thing," Clint added, "when I do come back for them, everything better be there."

"Oh," Eldon said, nodding his head, "everything will be there, all right."

"Good."

As Clint went out the door, Eldon called out, "Good luck," but he doubted that Clint Adams had heard him.

FIFTEEN

Clint stopped when he came within sight of the livery stable. It looked quiet and still. From the doorway he stood in, he figured he couldn't be seen. He had a few options, the most viable of which were to either sneak around to the back, or simply take them head-on.

He decided that he was tired of playing games. He was going to face them head-on, which would effectively take them by surprise.

He stepped out of the doorway and started for the stable. When he was within twenty-five feet of the front door he stopped.

"Sheriff!"

No answer.

"Come on, Sheriff," he called. "I know you're in there with Arch."

Still no answer.

"How many other cousins are in there with you?"

No reply.

He decided to just wait them out.

Quietly.

Inside the livery, four men were very nervous—none more than Sheriff Jack Pyle.

"Damn it!" he snapped. "How does he know we're in here?"

"He doesn't," Arch Pyle said. "He's bluffing."

"Well, what's he doin'?" Sam Irvin asked. He was a cousin to the Pyles, along with his brother, Stan, who was also in the livery. They were all watching from different vantage points, but Stan had the best view of Clint Adams, as he was looking right out the front door.

"Well, what's he doin', Stan?" Sam asked again, irritably.

"He ain't doin' nothin'," Stan Irvin said. "He's just standin' there."

"What do ya mean, he's just standin' there?" Sheriff Pyle asked.

"Just what I said, he's just standin' there, watchin'," Stan said.

"Stan," Arch said, "take a shot."

"What?"

Arch Pyle was above, in the hayloft. He, too, could see that Clint Adams was just standing out in the street, waiting for them to make the first move. Well, if that's what he wanted, that's what he was going to get.

"I said take a shot."

"Me?" Stan asked. "Why me?"

When Stan found out that it was Clint Adams
who had killed Dan Pyle, he had had second
thoughts about coming along on this ambush.
He had been with Dan the night before, when
he tried to kill Adams and got killed instead.
This morning, when Arch Pyle and his cousin,
the sheriff, told him and Sam what they were
going to do, the brothers had agreed to come
along. It was after that, though, when the Pyles
told the Irvins who the man was.

"Clint Adams?" Stan had asked. "That's the
Gunsmith, ain't it?"

"That's right," Arch had said, "it's the Gunsmith, but he's also the man who killed Dan."

That was good enough for Sam, but Stan was
still leery. Finally, they talked him into going
along.

Now Arch wanted him to take the first shot.

"I ain't takin' the first shot," he called back.

"Why not?" Arch asked.

"What if I miss?"

"You think he's gonna know who took the first
shot at him?" Arch demanded.

"Then you take the shot," Sam said, coming
to the aid of his brother.

"Jack?" Arch called.

"Take the shot, Arch," Sheriff Pyle said.

It never occurred to any of them that they
might fire all at once.

Clint kept his eyes on the front of the livery, waiting for some movement. He could hear
voices inside, but he couldn't make out what
they were saying. Suddenly, the door above the

main door, where they loaded in the hay, opened just a little, just enough for a gun barrel to slip out. He only saw it because he was watching so carefully.

He drew his gun and fired twice. He saw both bullets hit the door and go through. The next thing he knew the door flew open and a man fell to the ground.

"What happened?" Jack Pyle called.

"I don't know," Sam answered.

"Arch?" Sheriff Pyle called. "Arch?"

Stan Irvin looked out through the crack between the two big front doors and saw Arch Pyle lying on the ground. There was a lot of blood on him, and his neck was bent at a funny angle.

"He's dead, Jack!" he called out.

"What?"

"Arch is dead," Stan repeated. "He got shot and fell. He's lying in front of the doors." Stan turned and said, "His body's blocking the doors, Jack. We won't be able to open them."

"Damn it," Sheriff Jack Pyle swore. "What's Adams doin'?"

"What?"

"Adams. . . ."

Stan looked out through the crack between the doors again, but couldn't see Clint Adams.

"He's gone, Jack," he said. "Adams is gone."

SIXTEEN

When Clint saw the man's body hit the ground, he also saw that the body was blocking the front doors. He decided to make a run for the side of the stable before anyone else could react.

He made it to the side without a shot being fired. He paused only long enough to eject the spent shells from his gun and insert live ones. That done he pressed his back to the wall and moved along it until he came to the rear of the livery. He encountered no side door along the way, and he didn't know if there was one on the other side. When he got to the back he saw that the double doors there were closed, and likely locked from inside. He moved cautiously to them, hoping to get a look inside through a crack.

*   *   *

"Where is he?" Jack Pyle asked. "Anybody see him?"

The men were running around inside the stable, trying to see outside. They had covered the windows in anticipation of the ambush so they were looking for cracks in the walls or between doors to look out of.

"I don't see him," Sam Irvin called.

"Maybe we should uncover the windows," Stan suggested.

"No," Sheriff Pyle said. "No, don't do that."

Damn Arch, anyway, Jack Pyle thought. This was all his fault, and now he was dead and they were stuck with this situation.

"I'm gonna look out the back door," he called out.

"Don't open it!" Sam called.

"I'll look out the front again," Stan said.

Jack Pyle made his way to the back doors and put his right eye to the crack between them. What he saw made him go for his gun.

Clint made his way to the back doors and put his left eye to the crack to try to see inside. What he saw was another eye looking back.

"Jesus!" he heard a voice say, and he backed away and pumped two quick shots into the doors and, hopefully, through.

Jack Pyle jumped back, but he failed to move to one side or the other. Both of the shots fired by Clint Adams struck him in the torso, and he was dead before he hit the ground.

"Jack?" Sam Irvin called.

Sam ran to Jack's body and turned him over.

"Stan, Jack's dead."

"Well, hell," Stan said, "this was their fight and they're both dead. Why should we die, too?"

"You're right," his brother said. "Can you get the front door open?"

Stan pushed and the doors gave a bit.

"I think we both can," he said. "Come on."

Sam ran to the front of the livery, and he and his brother put their shoulders against the doors. Together they pushed them open, also pushing Arch Pyle's body out of the way.

As they stepped out of the stable, Clint Adams was standing there, covering them with his gun.

"Your voices carry pretty well," Clint said. He had heard them talking inside and had run around to the front to intercept them. "Drop your guns."

SEVENTEEN

When Scott Randolph rode into the town of Faith Hill, it had been almost two weeks since he'd met and then parted company with Clint Adams. When he got to January, Oklahoma, there was a telegram waiting for him from Adams, telling him to meet him here in Faith Hill, Texas. Because it had something to do with his wife, Randolph immediately turned around and headed back the way he had come until he reached Texas, and then headed for Faith Hill.

Now he left his horse at the livery stable and walked over to the hotel. Faith Hill was not a big town by any stretch of the imagination, and there was only the one hotel. He got himself a room and while signing the register checked for Clint Adams's name. Apparently, if Clint was in town he wasn't staying at the hotel.

"Can I do anything else for you, sir?" the clerk asked. "Someone to carry your bag?"

"No," Randolph said, "but I need a woman."

"Excuse me?" The clerk was a sandy-haired man in his fifties with prominent front teeth.

"A woman," Randolph said coolly, "I need a woman. Can you send one to my room?"

"Mister, we're not supposed—"

Randolph put five dollars on the countertop and said, "That's for you. Send a woman to my room."

"Uh . . . what kind?"

"Any kind," Randolph said, "as long as she's old enough."

Randolph went up to his room and set his saddlebags and rifle down. He walked to the window and looked outside. Every time he used a whore he hoped that his wife would understand that a man has needs. He never enjoyed it, but every so often a man needed a woman, and when he felt that urge, he just bought one, used her, and sent her away.

That's what whores were for.

He was sitting on the bed when there was a gentle, hesitant knock on the door.

"Come in."

The door opened and a woman came in. She saw him sitting on the bed, fully dressed, and stood half in and half out of the doorway.

"The clerk sent me up."

He didn't say anything.

"You did ask for a woman, didn't you?"

He still didn't answer.

She put her hands on her hips and asked, "What's the matter, I'm not good enough for you? You want me to leave?"

"No," he said, as she started to back out of the doorway. "Stay."

She smiled.

"Well, that's better."

She stepped into the room and closed the door. Her hair was so red it was disconcerting to Randolph. It was as red as Helen's.

"Well?" she asked. "How do you want it?"

He frowned.

"Slow? Fast? Dressed? Undressed?"

Randolph hesitated, then said, "Get undressed."

She nodded, reached behind her, undid a catch, and her dress fell to the floor. She wore no underwear. She had a sleek body, small breasts, slim waist, slender hips, wonderful skin. She had freckles on her breasts. He wondered idly if she also had them on her back. Helen had them on her back. Helen wasn't as slender as this woman, though. She was fuller in the breasts and hips. In fact, her hips were wide. She said she had her mother's childbearing hips. This woman was also younger than Helen, but she was about the same age Helen had been when they married.

She stood there for a moment with her hands on her hips, then frowned. The sight of her naked had most men panting to get their hands on her. Why was this one different?

"You're not undressing?"

Randolph cleared his throat.

"I think I made a mistake."

She stared at him for a moment and then shook
her head. He had the look. She was only in her
twenties, but she had been doing this long enough
to know the look—especially in men this man's
age. He needed a woman.

"What's your name?" she asked.

"Scott."

"Well, Scott, I don't think you made a mistake." She slid her right hand down over her
belly, into her pubic hair, and ran her middle
finger along her slit, moistening it. "Do you?"

He stared and found that he couldn't answer.
She could tell, though, by the bulge in his pants
that he agreed with her.

She walked to the bed and knelt down next to
him. He didn't move, and the smell of her tickled
his nose. She put her hands on his thighs and
rubbed him.

"Just relax," she said. "I'll do it all." She undid
his belt and said, "Leave it to Rita."

She undid his trousers. He already had his boots
unlaced so she was able to pull them off and toss
them into a corner. She pulled his underwear
off and his erection came into view. It wasn't
big, but it wasn't small, either. She touched her
fingers to the underside and it jumped. He was
smooth and hot, and swelling even more as she
touched him.

"Mmmm," she said, "you like me, I can tell
you like me."

He didn't say anything, just stared at her, at her
face, at her nipples, at her hand as it stroked him.

She leaned over then and ran her tongue along
the smooth underside of his penis. He moaned,

but kept his hands at his sides. She used her hand to raise his penis, opened her mouth, and took him inside. She was hot and wet, and she sucked him slowly. He felt himself responding, lifting his hips, feeling the rush in his loins. He put his hands on the smooth skin of her back, her neck, his eyes closed, enjoying the way her skin felt . . . and then he looked down and saw her head bobbing up and down, saw the red hair, the fiery red hair . . . and suddenly his penis went limp in her mouth.

She continued to work on him for a while, covering him with kisses, his thighs, his belly, sliding her hand beneath his testicles, doing everything she knew how to get him hard again, but nothing worked.

"That's it," she said, rocking back on her heels, "I give up. You're a hard man, Scott—I mean—"

"I know what you mean," he said. "It's not your fault."

"Well, that's a relief."

"It's my wife."

"Oh," she said, "you're married."

"Yes."

She stood up and picked up her dress.

"Where is she?" she asked, while putting it on.

"I don't know."

"You don't know?" She finished dressing and put her hands on her hips. "Did she leave you?"

"No." He put his feet on the floor and reached for his underwear and trousers. "She was taken."

"By who?"

"Apaches."

She stared at him and said, "Jesus."

He stood up and pulled on his trousers.

"When did that happen?"

"Ten years ago."

"And you still think about her?"

"I'm still looking for her."

Now her eyes widened.

"After all this time?"

"After all this time."

They stood there staring at each other.

"Um," she said, "before I go . . . do you want to try again?"

He took some money out of his pocket and said, "No."

EIGHTEEN

Clint rode into Faith Hill a lot later than he had expected. He'd wanted to arrive before Scott Randolph, and of course there was still a chance he had, but he still hadn't arrived when he'd wanted to.

After killing Sheriff Pyle he'd had to remain in Prairie Bend long enough to talk to a circuit judge. When one finally arrived Clint was the subject of a hearing. Luckily, the Irvin brothers testified on his behalf, hoping to make a deal for themselves.

He left town free and clear, and did not wait to see what kind of deal the Irvins did finally get.

He put Duke up at the livery and walked with his saddlebags and rifle to the hotel. When he entered he saw Scott Randolph sitting in the lobby. When Randolph saw him he rose and met him at the desk.

"About time," the older man said.

"I got held up, unavoidably," Clint said.

"How?"

"I killed a man."

"Anyone I know?"

"A sheriff."

"Ah," Randolph said, "I'm glad you didn't kill just anyone."

"I had to wait for a hearing."

"And were you cleared?"

"I'm here, aren't I?" Clint signed the register.

"And now that you are," Randolph said, "maybe you can tell me why I'm here?"

Clint turned and looked at Randolph.

"You're here to find your wife."

Randolph's eyes widened.

"You know where she is?"

"No," Clint said. "Come upstairs with me."

They went to Clint's room, and Randolph sat on the bed while Clint washed his face and hands with the water from a pitcher left on the dresser. He poured it into a basin, then rolled up his sleeves. When he was done he turned, towel in hand.

"I'll tell you what I heard," he said, "and you can tell me if you think I've called you here for a wild-goose chase."

Randolph listened while Clint told him what he'd learned from the man called Tanner. The man listened intently and didn't comment until he was done.

"Did you believe everything he said?"

"Why not?" Clint put the towel down and leaned against the dresser. "What did he have to gain by lying?"

"I don't know," Randolph said, "you tell me. You're the one who talked to him."

"He had nothing to gain," Clint said. "I didn't know him, and he didn't know me."

Randolph thought it over for a few moments.

"He saw red hair?"

"That's what he said."

"Well," Randolph said, "I've gone a lot further on less. Thanks for the information."

"Oh," Clint said, "I didn't come here just to bring you information."

"Why did you come?"

"To go with you."

"Why?"

Clint shrugged.

"Does it matter why?"

"Maybe not," Randolph said, "but I'm asking anyway."

Now it was Clint's turn to think a moment, and then he shrugged.

"I don't know why."

"Yes, you do."

"I'm nosy," Clint said, "and curious . . . and I want to help."

Randolph studied Clint for a few moments, then said, "Three pretty good reasons."

"You'll accept my help?"

"Sure," Randolph said, "why not? I've been doing it alone for ten years."

"Good," Clint said.

"We can get started in the morning," Randolph said. "I'll get the supplies."

"I've got some money—"

"Money's not a problem," Randolph said. "It never has been. In the beginning I used the money I saved, and the money I got for selling my land. After that I'd work whenever I needed money. Don't worry about money, Clint. You're helping enough."

"If this doesn't pan out—"

"Don't worry about that, either," Randolph said. "I've been down a lot of roads with no end before. If this is another . . ."

He shrugged his shoulders.

After Randolph left the room, Clint sat down on the bed and thought about the man's attitude. He was very calm about it all, but then he'd been at it for ten years. Still, he seemed too calm.

Clint wondered if it wasn't really the search the man wanted more now.

NINETEEN

While Randolph was still buying supplies Clint went to talk to the sheriff. He introduced himself, and Sheriff Andy Benson invited him to sit down. Benson was in his thirties, with the face and girth of a man ten years older, who had not taken good care of himself at all.

"What brings you to my town, Mr. Adams?"

It always amazed Clint how most town sheriffs thought that their badges meant that they owned the towns. How many times in the past had he heard men with badges refer to a town as "my town"?

"Apaches."

"Any Apaches in particular?"

"That's what I want to ask you," Clint said. "Has anyone seen a band of Apaches who had a white woman with them?"

"Well," the sheriff said, "wandering bands of Indians are seen all the time. Some of them are Apaches."

"Have you ever heard of a band that had a white woman with them?" Clint asked again. "A white woman with flaming red hair?"

"I haven't heard of anything like that myself," the sheriff said.

"Do you know of anyone who might have?"

Sheriff Benson shook his head.

"Not offhand, no."

"Would you mind if I asked around?"

"Why would I?" the lawman asked. "I appreciate you askin', though."

"Well," Clint said, standing up, "I wouldn't want to do anything wrong in . . . your town."

The sheriff smiled.

"I appreciate that."

Satisfied that he had done what was necessary with the sheriff, Clint stood up.

"Do you have any idea how long you'll be in town, Mr. Adams?" Andy Benson asked.

"Probably just overnight."

"What's your interest in these Apaches?" the lawman asked.

"My interest is not in the Apaches, Sheriff," Clint said, "it's with the woman."

"Do you think she's being held against her will?"

"I don't know anything, right now," Clint said, "except that she was taken against her will. What happened after that is anyone's guess."

Sheriff Benson frowned and asked, "Will you be, uh, expecting any assistance from me?"

"I doubt it, Sheriff." Clint saw the relief etched on the man's face and knew that the man would not have been much help anyway.

When Clint got back to the hotel, Randolph was in his room.

"We're set with supplies," the man told him.

"Good," Clint said. "I talked to the sheriff and he doesn't know anything that would help."

"What can we expect from him?"

"Nothing."

"That figures."

"Why don't we circulate around town and see if we can't find someone who will be of some help?"

"Good idea."

"We'll meet back here for dinner and compare notes," Clint said.

"Two hours all right?"

"Fine," Clint said.

"Only how about we meet at the saloon?" Randolph asked. "After talking to people for that long, I'll need a beer."

"The saloon it is, then," Clint said.

As they left Randolph's room he said, "I want to thank you in advance, Clint, whether we find her or not. I appreciate the help."

"I'm happy to do it, Scotty," Clint said, "only don't expect it for the next ten years, okay?"

TWENTY

Clint tried two different tactics. During the first hour he simply walked around town and kept his ears open. If there was any Apache activity going on in the area, he was sure that it would be the topic of someone's conversation. When he heard nothing, however, he spent the second hour asking questions. Some people looked at him suspiciously because he was a stranger, but others spoke freely. Unfortunately, most of the ones who spoke freely did not seem to have very much information.

Except one.

A man named Vincent Cates told Clint that he wanted to talk to a Virgil Ryan.

"Who's Virgil Ryan?"

Cates, a man in his fifties, was sitting in a chair in front of the saloon, whittling away at a chunk of wood which, at the moment, resembled nothing in particular. There were wood shavings at his feet and all around the chair, and also tobacco stains. Clint had walked to the saloon to meet Randolph and had run across Cates.

"Virgil knows more about Indians than anyone else around here," Cates said. "He's the one you want to talk to about Apaches."

"Where can I find him?"

"Well, now, that's a good question," Cates said. "He usually only comes into town when he needs supplies. He lives in the little shack just east of town, only about a half hour's ride."

"Just east of town, you say?"

"That's right."

"Will he talk to me?"

Cates glanced away from his hunk of wood and up at Clint, squinting against the sun.

"Well, that's another good question, ain't it?"

When Clint entered the saloon, Scott Randolph was not there yet. He got himself a beer and sat at a back table, nursing it while he waited. Activity in the saloon was in full swing, but that didn't mean much. There were no girls working the floor, and only one poker game going on. Other than that, men just seemed to be standing at the bar, or seated at tables, exchanging conversation and drinking, much for the same reason Vincent Cates was sitting outside whittling. Just to while away the hours.

Clint was halfway through his beer when Randolph appeared in the doorway. He looked around, saw Clint, and started directly for the table. Clint raised his beer, and Randolph stopped, detoured to the bar, got two beers, and walked over to the table.

"Thanks," Clint said. He drained the beer he'd been working on and then sipped the fresh one. "Find out anything?" he asked.

"Not much," Randolph said, "but somebody told me about a man we should talk to."

"Virgil Ryan?"

Randolph frowned.

"No," he said, "the name I got was Francis Healy."

"Who's he?"

"Well, from the description, he sounded like the town drunk, but I was told he knows a lot about Indians."

"That's what I was told about Ryan," Clint said, and went on to tell Randolph about the man—as much as he knew, anyway.

"Well, I guess we better talk to both of them," Randolph said.

"Let's split up again," Clint said. "You find Healy and I'll find Ryan."

"And we meet back here tonight?"

"Right," Clint said. "And I think we should get an early start in the morning."

"What if we don't find these fellas?"

"Then we'll find them tomorrow," Clint said.

"And if we don't then?"

"Well, then, I think we should just go out and try to find that tree. That would seem to be our starting point."

"I guess so."

Clint studied Randolph, who did not look all that optimistic. He wondered idly how many false roads the man had already been down in ten years. Was he already resigned that every time he found one it wasn't going to lead anywhere? And if so, why did he keep following them?

Maybe, Clint thought further, it's because it's all he can do.

"What's wrong?" Randolph asked.

Clint started and stared at Randolph and realized that the man had been studying him.

"Oh, nothing," Clint said. "I was just thinking about . . . oh, never mind."

"About all the other trails I've followed in the past ten years?"

"Well . . . yes."

"And you're wondering how I can keep doing it?"

Clint hesitated and said, "It's really none of my business."

"No," Randolph said, "it's just that, after all these years, if I stopped looking for her I don't know what I'd do with myself."

"Well, then," Clint said, after a moment, "let's go find her."

TWENTY-ONE

When Clint came within sight of Virgil Ryan's living quarters he realized that "shack" was a generous word for it. If this was, indeed, where the man lived, it was more a lean-to than anything else. It seemed to have three walls, with an opening where the fourth used to be. Obviously, that fourth wall had fallen down some time ago, and the roof was sagging in that direction.

"Hello!" Clint called out.

There was no answer.

He approached the "shack" and used the door to enter, even though a wall was missing. There was a table inside that seemed to fit in quite nicely, since it only had three legs. On the table was a plate that had been eaten off recently, but not cleaned out. It was covered with flies.

He stepped back out the door and looked around.

"Hello!"

No answer.

"I'm looking for Virgil Ryan!"

Seemingly from out of nowhere a voice called, "You found 'im. Who be you?"

Clint looked around, but he saw no one, and could not tell where the voice was coming from. There were trees and bushes around, and any number of things to hide behind, not the least of which were piles of old wood.

"My name's Clint Adams."

"What do you want with me?"

Still looking around, trying to locate the source of the voice, Clint said, "I want to ask you some questions."

"About what?"

"Apaches."

There was a long silence, and then the voice asked, "Who sent ya?"

"A man in town told me you know more about Apaches than anyone."

"Who was that?"

"Uh, his name was . . . Cates."

Another long silence, and then suddenly a man stepped out from a bush—not from behind the bush, but right from it. Apparently, the bush had a hollow center, which Clint doubted was natural.

The man approaching him looked to be in his sixties and was carrying an old Henry rifle. The prominent thing that Clint noticed about the man was his metal nose. That is, there was a piece of metal where his nose should have been. The metal seemed to be held on by a piece of string, much the same way an eye patch would have been.

The man advanced on Clint and stopped about two feet in front of him. When he stepped out of the bush the rifle was pointing at Clint. Now it pointed at the ground.

"See this?" the man asked, pointing to his own nose.

Clint could now see that he had a piece of a nose, and that the metal was covering a section that was missing.

"I see it."

"Apaches did this," Ryan said. "Tellin' you that I know more about Apaches than anybody else around here is Cates's idea of a joke."

"But *do* you know about them?"

The man squinted and said, "Son, I know about the ones that did this to me."

"Can I ask you some questions about them?"

"Sure."

"Thanks—"

"If'n you're willin' to pay," Ryan added. He shrugged and said, "A man's gotta eat."

"I don't have a problem with that."

"Then ask away."

"You want the money first?"

Ryan leaned his rifle against the front wall of his home and said, "I trust ya. Ask me the questions, and pay me what you think the answers are worth. That sound fair to you?"

"That sounds fair."

TWENTY-TWO

The man who told Randolph to seek out Francis Healy also told him to take a bottle of whiskey with him. Before leaving the saloon he bought a bottle—a cheap bottle—and then walked over to the livery. Apparently, when Healy wasn't at the saloon, he was sleeping at the livery stable.

"Francis?" the liveryman said. "Yeah, sure, he's in the back stall, on the right."

"Thanks," Randolph said.

He walked to the rear and as he approached heard someone snoring. Sure enough, he found a man sleeping on a bed of hay in the stall.

"Hey!"

The man snorted, but didn't awaken. The smell of stale whiskey hung over him like a cloud.

"Hey there!" Randolph said, and this time he nudged the man with his foot.

"Hey—wha—" the man said, coming blearily awake. He stared up at Randolph.

"I don't know you," he said, and closed his eyes to go back to sleep.

"Hey," Randolph said, this time with a light kick, "are you Healy?"

"Wha—"

The man opened his eyes again and gave Randolph the same bleary look.

"I don't know you," he said in the same tone of voice as before, but before he could close his eyes Randolph showed him the bottle in his hand.

"Hey!" the man said, coming fully awake. He reached for the bottle, sitting up, but Randolph pulled it back out of his reach.

"I want to ask you some questions," he said, "and then the bottle is yours."

Healy's eyes widened.

"The whole bottle?"

"That's right," Randolph said, "the whole bottle."

"What do ya wanna ask me?"

"I need to ask about Apaches in the area."

"We got 'em," Healy said, and reached. "Gimme the bottle."

"No, no," Randolph said, "I need more than that."

"Like what?" Healy was almost pouting.

"I need to know where to find them."

"They're all over!"

"I need to find a certain band of Apaches."

"Like who?" Healy asked. "Little Elk's band? Or Walking Bear's?"

"I don't know who," Randolph said. "All I know is that they have a white woman with them."

"There's a few of them with white women."

"A white woman with red hair."

Suddenly, Healy's eyes opened even wider and he skittered back on his butt until his back was against the wall.

"You know who I mean, don't you?"

"Hey, fella," Healy said, "you don't wanna find—"

"Yes, I do," Randolph said. "Who's the leader?"

The man didn't answer right away.

"Come on," Randolph said. He unstopped the bottle and added, "I'll pour this out on the ground if you don't answer."

"Don't do that!" Healy shouted, stretching his arms out.

"Then talk to me."

The man swiped the back of his hand over his dry mouth before answering.

"You want Pima Joe and his men."

"Pima Joe?" Randolph said. "I want Apaches, Healy, not Pima."

"They're not all Pima," Healy said. "Just Joe. The others are Apaches; Mescalero, Chiricahua, and others."

"Apaches and Pima? I thought—"

"They're outcasts from their own tribes," Healy said. "No one will have anything to do with them, so they all ride together."

"And they have a red-haired woman with them?"

"Yes," Healy said, "but she's Pima Joe's woman. You don't want to have anything to do with them."

"Yes," Randolph said, "I do. Where can I find them?"

"I don't know," Healy said. "They move around."

Randolph was about to hand the bottle of whiskey over when he thought better of it.

"Do you know of an odd-looking tree that's shaped like . . . like a circle?"

"Sure," Healy said. "The Indians call it the sun tree, because it's round."

"Can you tell me where to find it?"

"Sure," Healy said, "anybody can."

Randolph wondered why he and Clint had been asking about Indians and had not asked anyone about the damned tree.

"Give me directions and the bottle is yours," Randolph said.

"If you're going after Pima Joe," Healy said, "then I'm giving you directions to your own death."

"How do you know so much about Pima Joe and his men?" Randolph asked.

"Because," Healy said, looking away, "they have my wife."

TWENTY-THREE

"Pima Joe," Clint said. "That's what Virgil Ryan told me."

"Yeah," Randolph said, "but did Ryan say that Pima Joe had his wife, too?"

"No," Clint said, "only that Pima Joe had cut off most of his nose."

"What?"

Clint touched his nose and told him, "He's got a piece of metal covering it now."

"Jesus," Randolph said, "what must this animal have done to Helen?"

"Maybe nothing," Clint said, "if she's his . . . uh, woman."

"Yeah," Randolph said, wincing, "maybe. . . ."

"He also told me about the tree," Clint said. "The sun tree?"

"And how to find it?"

"Yes," Clint said. "It looks like we came up with the same information."

"I guess so."

"Except for one thing."

"What's that?"

"My guy will work for money," Clint said, "and not whiskey."

"Meaning what?"

"Meaning that if we pay him," Clint said, "he'll take us to the tree."

"I asked Healy about that," Randolph said. "He's too scared to go anywhere near Pima Joe."

"I guess I can understand that."

"I can't," Randolph said. "I can't understand how he can just leave his wife out there. I mean, he knows where his wife is. He could go and get her."

"And maybe get killed."

"I'm willing to take that chance."

"Well," Clint said, "obviously he can't."

"I don't have much respect for him, then."

"He lives inside a bottle, Scotty," Clint said. "How much respect can he have for himself?"

"I guess you're right."

They had met at the saloon again, but were now sitting in a nearby café, a steak in front of each of them. Clint's was almost gone, while Randolph's was still half intact.

"Come on," Clint said, "eat your steak, Scotty. Tomorrow we'll pick up Ryan at his shack and he'll take us to the tree. From there maybe we'll be able to track Pima Joe and his men."

"I can't wait," Randolph said, and then he pushed his plate away and added, "and I can't eat."

"Well, I can," Clint said. "Do you mind if I finish it? For some reason I'm starving."

"Go ahead," Randolph said. "Why should you starve because I can't eat?"

While Clint was finishing his steak, Randolph asked, "What's Ryan going to do after he shows us the tree?"

"I don't know."

"Do you think he'll help us track Pima Joe?"

"For enough money, probably."

"He's not scared?"

"To tell you the truth, I think he's too addled to be scared."

"But not too addled to show us the way to the tree?" Randolph asked.

Clint stopped eating.

"I guess addled is the wrong word."

"What's the right word, then?"

"I can't think of a word," Clint said. "I think he just doesn't care much anymore. I mean, look how he lives."

"He hid from you, didn't he?"

"Yes, but I don't think it was because he was scared," Clint said, "he was just being careful of a stranger."

"With that hollowed-out bush I guess he's careful of all strangers."

"So he's careful," Clint said. "So am I. It's how I've managed to stay alive this long."

"So you trust him?"

"I think if we pay him enough," Clint said, "we can trust him."

"How much is enough?" Randolph asked, looking worried.

"Don't worry," Clint said, "I doubt it will break us."

"Us?"

"Sure," Clint said, "I'll pay half and you pay half."

"Why should you pay half?"

"Why not?"

"It's my wife."

"It's my neck that will be on the line out there, right along with yours."

"And you're willing to pay for that?"

"Hey," Clint said, "you gave me your steak, right?"

Randolph stared across the table at Clint and shook his head.

"You're a good friend."

"Hey," Clint said, looking at Randolph, "after ten years I'd say you could use a friend, huh?"

TWENTY-FOUR

Clint was sitting on his bed, cleaning his guns, when there was a knock on his door. Thinking it must be Scott Randolph, he thought nothing of answering the door naked. When he opened it and saw a woman there they were both surprised.

"Oh," she said, in obvious surprise, but she didn't appear embarrassed at all. In fact, she looked him up and down very boldly.

Clint decided to be as bold. He stood there and examined her as well, liking what he saw. She was pretty, with black hair, pale skin, about thirty-five, with a full, womanly body.

"Can I help you?" he asked.

She was staring down between his legs and took her time moving her eyes back up to his.

"I'm here to help you," she said.

"How's that?"

"Your friend," she said, pointing, "in the next room? He sent me to . . . help you get to sleep?"

She smiled, a smile that revealed white teeth and transformed her from just pretty to very pretty.

"Did he?"

"Yes," she said, "but you don't look like the kind of man who has trouble sleeping."

"I'm not, usually."

"Well, then," she said, smiling even more broadly, "I guess he had something else in mind, didn't he?"

"I guess so."

She looked down at him again, and he did the same. They both saw that he was very interested in something other than sleeping.

"Are you going to let me in?"

"Oh yes . . ." he said, backing away from the door.

He woke the next morning and looked at the woman lying next to him. When she had entered the room the night before they had done very little talking. She had gone immediately to her knees and taken his erection lovingly into first her hands, and then her mouth.

After she sucked him for a while, she looked up at him and said, "You are definitely not interested in sleeping."

He pulled her to her feet and kissed her then, a long, wet kiss that made her moan deep in her throat. He began to undress her even before the kiss ended, and before long she was as naked as he—only more gloriously so.

Her body was indeed full, and he stared at her now, lying on her stomach, her buttocks so round and smooth, a wonderfully full butt that was firm and resilient. She was built exactly the way a woman should be built when her purpose in life—and her job—was to pleasure a man. While Clint did not usually use whores because he did not like to pay for sex, he was not adverse to having one in his bed when she was a gift.

Last night their sex had been frenzied. Apparently, his appearance at the door in the nude had excited her, just as her unexpected appearance had excited him. They had fallen onto the bed together, hands and mouths active and searching, and when he finally entered her, finding her wet and more than ready, they had pounded against each other so hard that they had caused the bed to move across the floor.

Later he pushed the bed back where it belonged and they made love again, a long, slow and satisfying dance this time. When he exploded inside her she began to buck beneath him, crying out, and if she was faking she was the best actress he had ever come across.

In fact, since her time was bought and paid for and he was immensely enjoying himself, he didn't care if she was acting or not.

But he didn't think she was.

Now he reached out and ran his hand over a butt he could only describe as "majestic." She stirred as he touched her, but didn't open her eyes. He slid his hand over her, his middle finger sliding along the crease between her cheeks. She moaned and spread her thighs so he could reach down further until he found her, wet and warm, ready and waiting.

He slid over her from behind and she spread her legs wider so he could enter her from behind.

"Ooh, oh . . ." she said, and took two handfuls of sheet as he started to move in and out of her. "Oh God, oh yes, ooh . . ."

As his strokes became faster and faster she moved up onto her knees and began to rock back against him. He took hold of her hips, then, and began to slam into her so that they could hear when his belly slapped against her butt.

"Oh yes, oh, Clint, oh damn . . ." she moaned and cried out.

Finally he felt that rush come up from inside him and he couldn't hold it back. As he exploded inside her, she grabbed ahold of the headboard and pushed back against him, grinding against him. . . .

"I'm sure glad you weren't looking for help sleeping," she said as she dressed. "I would hate to have missed any of that."

"Me, too."

He was lying on his back, watching her dress. Although it was morning it was still dark out, but she said she had to get back to her place and get some real sleep.

"I'll look like a scarecrow if I don't," she said.

"Never."

She smiled and said, "You're sweet."

She walked to the bed, leaned over, and kissed him deeply.

"Are you leaving today?" she asked.

"I am."

"Too bad."

"I know."

"Coming back?"

"I might."

"You come and see me," she said. "We'll do this again."

"But—"

"Free of charge, of course," she added, and stroked his cheek.

He watched her go out the door, then got up to wash and dress himself and go downstairs to meet Scott Randolph and check out.

After thanking him for his gift, of course.

TWENTY-FIVE

When Clint got to the lobby, Scott Randolph was already there, waiting.

"I heard you wake up this morning," Randolph said, with a smirk. "That is, I heard your present wake up."

"I have to thank you for that gift, Scott," Clint said. "It wasn't necessary, but I'm sure glad you went ahead and did it anyway."

"Yes," Randolph said, "I could tell by the noise that you were both enjoying yourselves."

"Sorry if we kept you awake," Clint said. He was about to say something else but thought better of it. He was going to ask, half joking, if Randolph had given himself a similar gift, but seeing as how the man was on a ten-year quest—so far—to find his wife, he didn't know what the man was doing about things like sexual urges.

"I don't sleep that well in hotels, anyway," Randolph said. "It gave me something to do while I waited for the sun to come up."

Clint remembered that the man had slept fairly well that night on the trail. It was odd to think that he slept better on the ground than in a bed—and yet, understandable. He had probably spent most of the past ten years sleeping on the ground.

They checked out and paid their bills, and then headed for the livery.

"Does this fella Ryan have a horse?"

Clint stopped short.

"You know, I didn't ask him."

"Maybe we'll have to buy him a horse, as well as pay him for his services."

"If he doesn't have one," Clint said as they started walking again, "we can rent him one. I don't think we have to buy him one."

They got to the livery and waited while their horses were saddled for them.

"Do you know Virgil Ryan?" Clint asked the man when he came out with their horses.

"Sure," the man said, "everybody knows ol' Virg."

"Do you know if he has a horse?"

"He sure does, a broken-down ol' nag that he shoulda shot a long time ago."

"Is it here?"

"Hell, no," the man said, "Virg thinks his horse is too good to leave here for me to take care of."

Clint detected a note of hurt feelings or battered pride in the man's voice.

"I see," Clint said. "Thanks."

"If he did leave that nag here," the man went on as Clint and Randolph mounted up, "I'd sell her for her bones, I would."

"Thanks," Clint said again.

The man was still muttering as they rode away.

"At least we know he's got a horse," Clint said.

"Doesn't sound like much of a horse," Randolph said. "I hope he can keep up with us."

"Oh, it just sounded like hurt feelings to me," Clint said. "I'll bet the horse is just fine."

As Clint and Randolph approached Virgil Ryan's shack, Clint said, "This is the place."

"I could guess," Randolph said. "What's that in front of the place?"

"What's what?" Clint asked.

"That . . ." Randolph said, " . . . that thing standing in front of the place."

The only thing Clint saw standing in front of the shack was a gray swaybacked mare that had seen better days.

"That's a horse, Scott," Clint said.

"That," Randolph asked, "is a horse?"

TWENTY-SIX

Virgil Ryan's swaybacked mare turned out to be a surprise. Not only was she keeping up with Clint's and Randolph's horses but at times she seemed to be doing even better than they were.

"That's an odd-looking horse you've got there, Mr. Ryan," Randolph had commented.

"The way she looks got nothin' to do with the way she rides...and you don't have to call me mister. Just call me Virgil. Everybody does."

"All right, Virgil."

Clint remembered that Tanner's estimate of how far the tree was from Faith Hill was about a day and a half's ride. They were a few miles outside of town when he asked Ryan how accurate that was.

"I guess that would depend on how much horse you got under you," Ryan said.

While Ryan's horse certainly did have more stamina than she appeared to, Clint doubted that she had more speed.

"You figure it'll take us about a day and a half?" he asked.

"I figure," Virgil said. Then he added, "Unless we run into ol' Pima Joe before that."

"Virgil," Randolph said, "you mind me asking why Pima Joe, uh, cut off the tip of your nose?"

"Wasn't the tip," Ryan said, "was almost the whole thing . . . and no, I don't mind you askin'."

Randolph waited for more, but when none was forthcoming he figured that while Ryan didn't mind him asking, he apparently minded answering.

"You think we might run into him between here and the tree?" Clint asked.

"Him, or some of his men, or maybe nobody. You know, the Indians ain't never seen a tree like this. They like to camp near it, but they're afraid to go too near it. They think the Sun God made it the way it is."

"Why?"

"'Cause they can't figure out how it coulda growed that way."

"No," Randolph said, "I mean why do they think—what purpose do they think the Sun God had in mind?"

"Damned if I know," Ryan said.

During the course of the first half day's ride they continued to make conversation with Virgil

Ryan, who never seemed to mind talking. Sometimes, though, he just wouldn't answer a question if he didn't feel like it, and they learned not to take offense.

"Virgil, what do you know about a man named Francis Healy?" Randolph asked.

"What do I got to know about him?"

"Do you know him?"

"Yeah, I know him."

"I understand that Pima Joe has his wife—at least Healy says that he does."

"You don't believe him?"

"I just have a hard time believing that a man could lose his wife to some Indians and then forget about her," Randolph said.

Ryan looked at him then, which was unusual. He had done most of his talking and answered most of the questions without moving his eyes from what was ahead.

"You think he lies in a horse stall with a snootful of whiskey because he forgot her?"

"I guess—"

"That ain't hardly likely."

Randolph fell silent for a moment, then said, "I guess I wasn't thinking."

"How long ago was his wife taken?" Clint asked.

"Couple of years, I reckon."

"Is she Pima Joe's?"

"Hell, no," Ryan said, "Pima's squaw would cut the tits off'n any other woman he wanted."

"His white squaw?" Clint asked, feeling Randolph stiffen in his saddle.

"That's right," Ryan said.

"She's got red hair, right?"

"That's right. We talked about that, didn't we?"

"Yes," Clint said. He was riding between Ryan and Randolph and at that moment studiously avoided turning to look at the latter man. He didn't want to see the anguished look on Randolph's face. He had seen it too many times already.

"Yes," he said, "we talked about that."

"She yours?" Ryan asked.

"No," Clint said, "she was never mine."

Ryan looked at Randolph as he rode ahead of them a ways.

"His?" the old man asked, jerking his head in Randolph's direction.

"She was his, at one time."

"How long?"

"Ten years."

Even the usually stoic Ryan showed surprise at that.

"He's been lookin' for his woman for ten years?"

"That's right."

Ryan rubbed his jaw.

"She ain't been his woman for a long time now, you know that, don't you?"

"I think so."

"Even if we find Joe and his men, she ain't gonna wanna leave."

"I think I know that, too."

"You think he knows it?"

"I don't know, Virgil," Clint said, studying Randolph's back. "I think he's concerned with finding her. I don't think he's given all that much thought to what will happen when he does."

"I guess not," Ryan said. "If he had, we wouldn't be out here right now."

TWENTY-SEVEN

They went through the day without any sign of Apaches, or any other kind of Indians. When they camped they divvied up the chores. Clint saw to the horses and Randolph collected wood for the fire. That left Virgil Ryan to cook, and he was remarkably good at it, considering the way he lived.

When both Clint and Randolph exhibited their surprise, Ryan said, "Just 'cause I live like a slob don't mean I can't cook."

"No, I guess not," Clint said.

Not only was the food good, but the coffee was true trail coffee, hot and as black as it could be. Whoever Virgil Ryan was and whatever he had done during his life before he had had his nose cut off and took to living in a three-walled shack, he had spent time on the trail sometime in his life.

After they finished eating, Ryan said, "I suggest we stand watch. You never know when a band of those Indians will creep up on you. I don't cotton to wakin' up some mornin' with my throat cut and my tongue hangin' out the cut like some kinda necktie."

"Jesus," Randolph said, "that sounds horrible."

"It is," Ryan said. Then he shivered and added, "I hate neckties."

Clint took the first watch after making sure that Ryan made another pot of coffee. He drank it slowly, staring out into the dark, being sure not to look directly into the fire. With any luck, by midday the next day they should find the tree. He wondered what would happen after that. Would there be any kind of trail they could follow? And even if there were, it was certainly possible that the trail would not be made by Pima Joe and his men.

Also, what would Virgil Ryan do at that point? Continue on with them—for more money, of course—or turn around and head back to Faith Hill? Would they even need him after that?

Clint turned quickly when he felt someone behind him. It was Randolph.

"Can't sleep?"

"No. Any of that coffee left?"

"Help yourself."

Randolph hunkered down and poured himself a cup of coffee, then sat across the fire from Clint.

"I thought you said you slept better on the trail?" Clint asked.

"I do," Randolph said, "but then I hardly sleep on the trail, either."

"I see," Clint said. "Maybe we should have just let you stand watch the whole night."

"I've done it before," Randolph said, sipping his coffee. "You can turn in if you like. I had the second watch anyway. I can just start it early."

"That's okay," Clint said. "I'm really not ready to go to sleep yet."

They sat in silence for a while and then Randolph asked a question that surprised Clint.

"Ever been married, Clint?"

He hesitated a moment and then said, "No. Came close once, but..." He let it trail off.

"What happened?"

Apparently, Randolph wasn't going to let him off the hook.

"She died," Clint said. "That is, she was killed."

Randolph stared at him a few moments.

"Well," he said, "that makes what I was going to say sound foolish."

"Why?"

"I was going to say that you can't know what I'm going through—"

"You'd be right, though," Clint said. "I can't. What happened to me was a long time ago, and it was over very quickly."

"True," Randolph said. "My... ordeal does seem to be lingering, doesn't it?"

"Well," Clint said, "maybe we can do something about that over the next few days."

"I hope so," Randolph said, shaking his head. "Just between you and me, I'm starting to get a little tired."

Well, is it any wonder? Clint thought.

TWENTY-EIGHT

When Clint saw the tree, he stopped and stared at it. Next to him, Randolph was also staring. Virgil Ryan, on the other hand, was looking around them, alert for the appearance of any Indians. It was past midday. It had taken them a little longer than they figured to get there.

After a few moments Ryan said, "You just want to stare at it?"

Clint looked at him and said, "No. Let's have a look around."

The tree was on a small rise, and at the base of it on the other side was an area that had obviously been used again and again as a campground. The camp was bare now, but there were some ashes where the fire had been.

Before going down to the campsite they looked again at the tree.

"Oddest thing I ever saw," Clint said.

"You said it," Randolph agreed.

The trunk of the tree came up out of the ground and then suddenly split in two, went up and over and then met, forming a circle.

"It just naturally grew this way?" Clint asked.

"Can you figure out how somebody could *make* it grow this way?" Ryan asked.

Clint just shook his head.

They rode down to the camp. Ryan dismounted and went to the ashes.

"How recent, Virgil?" Clint asked.

"A couple of days," Ryan said, dusting off his hands. He looked around and then pointed. "They went in that direction."

Clint nodded and looked at Randolph.

"It's your call," he said. "Do we follow this trail?"

"There's no guarantee it's their trail," Randolph replied.

"I know," Clint said, "but it's the only trail we have."

"And if it's the wrong one?"

"We'll deal with that when the time comes," Clint said. "What do you say?"

Randolph looked around once, then back at Clint.

"Let's follow it."

"Ryan?" Clint asked. "What are you going to do?"

Ryan stared up at them, stroking his stubbly chin. The sun reflected off the piece of metal that was hiding his nose—or what was left of it.

"You fellas would probably get killed without me," he said finally.

"How much?" Clint asked.

"No extra money," Ryan said, mounting up.

"What?"

"I figure after all these years this fella deserves a chance to find his wife," the old man said. "I'll just throw this in as extra."

"Extra," Randolph said.

"Yeah," Ryan said, "that's right."

"What happens if we find the Indians who made these tracks and it's Pima Joe and his men?" Clint asked.

Ryan shrugged.

"Damned if I know," he said. "I guess we'll find out when we find them."

"Can you tell anything from the tracks?" Clint asked.

"Naw," Ryan said. "They're just unshod ponies. All I know is that they were definitely made by Indians."

"What about footprints?" Randolph asked.

Ryan waved his arm and said, "They trampled all over each other."

"We're just going to have to follow the trail and see where it leads us," Clint said.

"Agreed," Randolph said.

"Let's go, then," Ryan said. "We still got a few hours of daylight and we sure don't wanna be camped here if somebody comes along."

TWENTY-NINE

Pima Joe had learned much over the years about the way the white men did things—also, the way white women did things.

Like sex.

He had learned something about himself, too, at a very early age. He craved white women. He liked the way their skin looked, and the way they had different color hair. Later in life he became enamored of both blond hair and red hair, and ten years ago, when he got the chance to steal a red-haired white woman, he took it.

Now her red hair was down between his legs, doing things to him that an Indian woman would never do. Indian women did not even kiss, and his red-haired white woman was doing much more now with her mouth than just kissing.

She sucked him wetly, knowing that was the

way he liked it, and he put his head back and enjoyed the sensations her mouth was causing. When he was perilously close to exploding she released him with her mouth and scrambled into his lap, lowering herself onto his rigid penis.

They were on a blanket in his shack—he preferred a wooden shack to a tipi—and he was in a seated position so that they were facing each other as she rode up and down on him. He slid his hands beneath her to cup her buttocks, which were slick with her wetness. He stared into her face and noticed, again, the lines at the corners of her eyes and mouth. She was getting older, and maybe it was time to find a new woman, a younger one. After all, she was older even than he was. He knew that when he first took her she was in her middle twenties, while at the time he was only nineteen. Now he was a full grown man of twenty-nine, in his prime, and she was in her middle thirties and beginning to show some wear.

As he felt an explosion building in his loins he also realized that she knew what he liked, and was not shy about doing it. Of course, it had taken time for her to reach that point, and if he went out and stole another white woman, it would take time for her to learn as well.

He wanted to give it some more thought, but the time for that was later. Suddenly, he was erupting inside her, and she was raking his back with her nails, biting his shoulder, and he was squeezing her buttocks tightly in his big hands, and they were both crying out loud and riding waves of pleasure that went on and on and on. . . .

* * *

    Later, while she slept, Pima Joe stared down at
her and continued his thoughts. Maybe he could go
out and get another white woman and this one—
who had been called Helen when he stole her, but
had been called Fire Hair since then—could teach
her what she needed to know to please him. After
that, he could keep both of them or send Fire Hair
on her way, or give her to one of the other braves
who he knew lusted after her.

    He stood up and walked to the front door.
Naked, he opened it and stared out. He was a
big man, sturdily built, thick through the middle
but not fat, standing well over six feet in height.
Outside he saw camp fires in front of tipis, women
cooking for their men. All but one of the other
women in camp were Indian, but the other white
woman had black hair, like the squaws, and her
skin had grown dark from the sun. He did his best
to keep his Fire Hair inside, away from the sun,
because he loved her pale, freckled skin. When he
had first taken her he didn't know how her skin
would react to the sun. She had become burned
and her skin had peeled away like the hide of an
animal, or the shed skin of a snake. After that
he kept her away from the sun, and her skin had
gone back to its former paleness.

    As he stood naked in the doorway some of the
other women examined him admiringly. He knew
there were any number of women in the camp who
lusted after him, but he was not interested in Pima
women, or Apache women, or any Indian women.
Eventually, he backed away from the door and
closed it. Behind him Fire Hair stirred and sat up,

running her long, pale fingers through her hair.

"What is it?" she asked.

"Nothing."

She spoke his tongue with an odd accent that he didn't like, and so when they were alone they spoke in the white man's language. It used to anger him that she could not learn to speak his language fluently, but he had finally given up on that.

"You are restless," she said.

"Perhaps."

Her eyes roamed over his body and then she reached for him and said, "Come back and lie with me."

"No," he said firmly, "I must go and talk to the others."

"About what?"

He donned his leather leggings and glared at her.

"It is for men to know, not for you."

She stuck her lower lip out in a pout she knew he liked. That is, he had liked it when she was younger, but lately he thought she looked silly doing it.

He picked up his holster and strapped it on. Six years ago he had decided that the white man's pistol was the best weapon to wear, and he had become very efficient with it. Now he never went anywhere without it.

"I will be back later," he said, and went out the door without another word.

After Pima Joe was gone she stood up and walked to one of the front windows naked. She would have gotten dressed, but he liked to come back and find her naked.

She had been with him ten years and could hardly remember a time when she wasn't with him. Those early days of her capture, when she was resisting him and he would beat her, were a dim memory. And the days before that, when she lived with her husband, were hardly a memory at all. Sometimes, at night, she would dream about those days, but even when she was awake they seemed like a dream. Sometimes, she could hardly remember her white name . . . Helen.

She could hardly remember what her white husband looked like, and when she tried to think about it her head hurt. Also, if Pima Joe ever found her looking pensive he would get angry with her, thinking that she was trying to remember her former life.

She watched out the window as women cooked, and made clothes, and did laundry, and wished that Pima Joe would let her join them. She had no friends because she was Pima Joe's woman, and even when she did go out among them they hardly spoke to her.

She rubbed her arms and turned away from the window and suddenly, as if she had been struck by a physical blow, she staggered as a face came into her mind. It was sharp and clear and it shocked her so, because she had not seen him that clearly in many years.

It was the face of her white husband, Scott Randolph.

THIRTY

Clint found that when they camped for the night Virgil Ryan had very little trouble getting to sleep. Randolph, on the other hand, slept very little, and Clint was somewhere in the middle.

Once again he and Randolph found themselves sitting up around the camp fire while Ryan snored away behind them.

Along the way the tracks they were following had started to tell their story. Once away from the campground by the tree they cleared up, and it became obvious that these particular tracks were made by six different ponies. The interesting thing was that five of them were unshod, and the sixth was shod. What they had to continue to hope was that these six riders were part of Pima Joe's band, and that their tracks would lead right to him.

"I'll be surprised if they do, though," Ryan had said, before turning in.

"If they belong to his men?" Randolph asked.

"No," Ryan said, "if they lead us to him. Pima Joe is not that careless."

"There's always a first time," Randolph said.

"Would any white man—uh, without a badge and a posse, that is—in his right mind be looking for Pima Joe and his men?" Clint asked.

Ryan chuckled.

"I don't even think a man with a badge would follow the trail."

Randolph looked at Clint and Ryan and said, "I guess that makes us pretty brave, huh?"

"Brave," Ryan said, "stupid . . . or mad."

"Which one are you?" Clint asked.

"Well," Ryan had said, rolling himself up in his blanket, "I ain't brave."

Now Clint and Randolph sat across the fire from each other, drinking Ryan's trail coffee.

"I wonder if there are any towns around here," Randolph said.

"I don't think Pima Joe would be camping anywhere near a town," Clint said, "but we can ask Ryan in the morning."

"I was just wondering."

Clint looked up at Randolph and found the man staring into the fire.

"Scott!"

"Huh?"

"Don't look into the fire," Clint said. "You'll destroy your night vision."

"Oh," Randolph said, abruptly averting his eyes, "I didn't even realize I was doing it."

"What were you thinking?"

Randolph rubbed his eyes with his hands and blinked them several times before answering.

"Every so often," he said, "I find that I . . . I can't remember what my wife looks—looked like."

"It's been a long time, Scott," Clint said. "Maybe you shouldn't remember what she looks like."

Randolph frowned and asked, "Why not?"

"Because she's probably not going to look like that when you find her."

Randolph stared at Clint for a few moments, then nodded his head and said, "I've thought about that—believe me, I've thought about that. What do I do if I don't recognize her at all? Or worse, what if she doesn't recognize me?"

"Scott," Clint said, "what if she doesn't want to go back with you? Have you thought about that at all?"

"I've thought about everything," Randolph said. "Over the past ten years I've had every thought you can imagine—except I haven't ever been able to think about not looking for her."

"Scott—"

Randolph waved Clint's words away.

"I think you should turn in, Clint," he said. "It's my watch, and I need the time to think."

Clint nodded and walked to his bedroll. He wondered how many times, over and over again, Randolph had thought about the same things over the past ten years.

He thought that, given the same set of circumstances, if he were the husband who had been looking for his wife for ten years, he'd probably be mad by now.

He both admired and felt sorry for Scott Randolph.

THIRTY-ONE

Clint came awake abruptly, certain that something was wrong. As he reached for his gun, a moccasin clad foot came down on his wrist just hard enough to pin it to the ground. He looked up and saw an Indian glaring down at him.

"Sorry, Clint," Scott Randolph said, "I guess I was thinking too hard. They sneaked up on me."

Clint looked around and saw that there were five Indians in camp. One of them was standing by Randolph, training a rifle on him. Three others were standing around, watching. The fifth, of course, was standing on his wrist. He strained his eyes further to see what Virgil Ryan was doing; the old man appeared to still be asleep.

"Get up," the Indian who was standing on Clint's hand said to him.

The brave removed his foot and Clint slowly stood up. He was no expert on Indians, but the five seemed to be from mismatched tribes.

When he was standing all seven of them turned their attention to Ryan, who was still wrapped in his blanket, seemingly asleep.

"What do you want?" Clint asked.

"Quiet!" one of the braves snapped. It was the one who had stood on his wrist. Apparently he was the leader. He looked at one of the other braves, waved his arm toward Ryan, and said, "Wake him."

"He's just an old man," Clint said. "He can't hurt you."

The brave backhanded Clint across the face and said again, "Quiet." He looked at his man and repeated, "Wake him."

The other brave nodded and walked over to where Ryan was sleeping. As he bent over with a knife to wake the man, Ryan's blanket seemed to burst into flame and there was the sound of a shot—or maybe it was the other way around. Anyway, the brave bending over him staggered back under the force of the blow. The other Indians were surprised, and Clint sprang into action. He dove to the ground for his gun, grabbed it, and came up shooting. He shot one Indian in the chest and another in the shoulder as the brave fled.

Scott Randolph was the last to move, grabbing his gun from the ground and firing at the fleeing Indians. He didn't know if he'd hit any of them.

Ryan sprang from the smoking blanket, cackling like a madman and bouncing around.

"An old man, huh? Can't hurt ya, huh? I showed 'em. They ran like scared rabbits."

"Yes, they did," Clint said, "but they left something behind."

The something they had left behind was two dead braves.

"Are these Pima Joe's men, Virgil?" Clint asked.

"Wait," the old man said. He bent over both men, examining them. "I can't tell. I don't recognize them, and his men don't have any special markings."

"Great," Clint said. "They were probably just a—"

"I did recognize a voice, though," Ryan said abruptly, "or I think I did."

"A voice?"

He nodded. "The one who was giving the orders."

"Yeah," Clint said, touching his face, "he hit me."

"Well, his voice sounded familiar," Ryan said, "like somebody who was there when they did this to me." He indicated his nose.

"Well," Clint said, "of the three that got away at least one was wounded. I don't think they'll be coming back here. Let's drag these two out of camp."

Randolph and Clint did that, and as they were walking back Randolph said, "I'm really sorry, Clint."

"It's okay."

"I almost got us killed."

"We're not dead," Clint said, "that's what counts."

"Yeah, but I let them walk right into camp," Randolph said. "I was careless."

"We all get careless sometimes, Scott."

Randolph shook his head, unwilling to accept that as a way out.

"No," he said, "I think maybe I've been at this too long."

"Maybe it's time to go back to ranching," Clint said, "or maybe you just need a bit of a rest."

"A bit of a rest?" Randolph asked. "From a ten-year quest?"

"Why don't you wait until this part of it is over to decide what to do?" Clint suggested. "Ryan and I will go back to sleep, and you continue your watch."

Randolph stared at him.

"You're willing to let me go back on watch after what happened just now?"

"Hey," Clint said, "I don't think you're going to get careless again tonight, do you?"

"Hell no!" Randolph said.

"Then you're the best candidate to stand watch, aren't you?"

THIRTY-TWO

The rest of the night passed without incident, and they had breakfast together when Ryan woke Clint and Randolph at first light. Surprisingly enough, Randolph had actually fallen asleep after Ryan had relieved him for watch. It was decided that the old man would always take the third watch, because he was going to prepare breakfast in the morning.

"Tell me something," Randolph said to Ryan, "how'd you know what was going on?"

"I smelled 'em."

"Smelled them?"

Ryan nodded.

"Earlier in the evenin'."

"You mean . . . you knew there were Indians out there?" Randolph asked.

"Sure I did," Ryan said, "I was just wonderin'

when they was gonna come in."

"And you didn't tell us anything?"

"First of all," Ryan said, "you might not have believed me, and second of all if you did, you mighta been kinda jumpy. This way you acted natural, they came in, and I got the drop on 'em, didn't I?" He finished by cackling, and as he did so some food fell from his mouth to the ground.

"You sure did, Virgil," Clint said. "You saved our lives."

"Bet you're glad I decided to stay with you, huh?" Ryan asked.

"I know I am," Clint said.

"I still think you should have told us what was happening," Randolph grumbled.

"Would you have moved any faster than you did if I had?" Ryan asked.

It was an obvious crack about Randolph being the last to move when Ryan fired his gun from beneath the blanket.

"You always sleep with your gun under the blanket?" Clint asked, trying to get in between them before they could start an argument.

"Most of the time, yeah," Ryan said. "Something happens to a man when he loses a piece of his body, ya know?" He moved a finger to his nose and almost touched it. "I ain't about to let nothin' like this happen to me again."

"Let me ask you something, Virgil," Clint said.

"Ask away."

"Are you out for revenge for what Pima Joe did to your nose?"

"Not really," Ryan said, "but if the chance comes, why not?"

"And you think the chance will come with us?"

Ryan squinted at Clint.

"I know who you are, ya know."

"I introduced myself to you."

"No," the old man said, "I mean I know who you really are."

"And who is that?"

"The Gunsmith," Ryan said. "You got as big a rep as Wild Bill Hickok ever had. If anybody can bring Pima Joe down, it's gonna be you. I don't mind tellin' you I'd like to be there when it happens."

"Well," Clint said, "I hate to disappoint you, but I'm not here to bring down Pima Joe, I'm here to help my friend find his wife."

Ryan shook his head, cackled, and said, "It amounts to the same thing."

"Why do you say that?" Randolph asked.

Ryan looked at him.

"If Pima Joe's red-haired white woman turns out to be your wife, and you want her back," he explained, "the only way you're gonna do it is to kill Pima Joe."

"And you intend to help us, if it comes to that?" Randolph asked.

Ryan spread his hands and said, "I'm here, ain't I . . . and I already saved your bacon once."

Before Randolph could say anything, Clint said, "That you did, Virgil. That you most certainly did."

THIRTY-THREE

About a hundred yards from where they had camped they found the place where the five Indians had left their horses.

"Two of the horses wandered off without riders," Ryan said. "The other three went west."

There was also blood on the ground, but not enough to indicate that more than one man was wounded.

"What about the trail we've been following?" Randolph asked.

"It's gettin' colder."

Randolph looked at Clint.

"Do you think we should follow this new trail?"

"I think we've got as good a shot with this new trail as with the old one to find Pima Joe," Clint said. "What do you think, Virgil?"

"There's a track here that looks familiar," the old man said.

"From where?"

"From the trail we started to follow." The old man stood up and faced them. "I think both of these trails have a pony in common."

"So one man was involved in leaving both trails," Clint said.

"Maybe."

"Well," Clint said, "maybe or not, it makes our decision a lot easier. We'll follow this new trail, Virgil."

"Whatever you say," Ryan said, mounting up. "Let's go."

They rode for half a day, following the trail of the three ponies, when they spotted something on the ground ahead of them.

"Looks like a body," Ryan said.

Sure enough when they reached it, it was the body of an Indian and he'd been shot.

"He's got a bad shoulder wound," Ryan said, examining the fallen man. "Looks like he bled to death."

They had been seeing blood on the ground all along the trail. Apparently, the Indians had done nothing to try to stem the flow of blood. Finally, when the man fell from his horse, the others just left him.

Ryan stood up.

"His pony wandered off that way," he said, pointing south. "The trail is now bein' made by two ponies."

Randolph looked at Clint.

"If they split up, we'll have to split up, too," he said.

"Maybe they won't be that smart," Clint said. "Let's keep moving, Virgil."

"You don't want to stop to eat?" Ryan asked, looking disappointed.

Clint shook his head.

"That'll just give them more of a head start," he said. "If possible I want to catch up to them before they get where they're going."

"Why?" Randolph said. "Wouldn't it be better for them to lead us to the camp?"

"I think it would be better if we catch them and make them tell us about the camp," Clint said. "We don't want to ride into the camp blind."

"Wait a minute," Ryan said, mounting up and moving his horse up alongside them. "Did you say we were goin' to ride into camp?"

"What else would we do?" Clint asked.

"That's suicide."

"Will they kill us on sight?" Clint asked. "Or will they want to hear what we have to say?"

Ryan hesitated.

"See," Clint went on, "they don't know we're hunting them. They'll assume we're just drifting."

"Not with me along you ain't," Ryan said.

"Will they recognize you?" Randolph asked.

"They'll recognize this," Ryan said, pointing to his nose.

"Okay," Clint said, "so when we reach the camp Randolph and I will ride in. We'll look around and see if we can spot his wife."

"And if not?" Ryan asked.

"Then we get out of there as soon as possible."

Ryan didn't look as if he liked that, but he kept it to himself if he didn't.

"And if she is there?" he asked.

"Then we'll have to figure out a way for Randolph to talk to her and see if she wants to leave with him."

"See if she'll even recognize me," Randolph said glumly.

"That, too," Clint said. He looked at Ryan and continued, "Before we can do any of that, though, we've got to find the camp, and I think catching up to these last two Indians before they get there will be the best way to go."

"Then we better keep movin'," Ryan said. He pulled a piece of beef jerky from his pocket and popped it into his mouth. "I got *my* lunch."

THIRTY-FOUR

"We're not gonna catch up to them."

Clint looked down at Ryan, who got back to his feet and looked up at him.

"Why not?" Clint asked.

"We're not gaining on them."

"Are we losing ground?"

"No," Ryan said. "We're stayin' even with them."

Clint exchanged a glance with Randolph.

"Will they travel at night?" Randolph asked Ryan.

The old man scratched the stubble on his face.

"I don't think so."

"Can we?" Clint asked.

Ryan hesitated, then said, "I can." He looked at Clint. "I think you can, especially with that horse." He looked at Randolph then. "I don't know about you."

"Don't worry about me," Randolph said. "I've traveled at night before."

"We'll just stay behind you, Virgil," Clint said. "We'll step where you step. Are you willing?"

"Hell, I'm willin' to do anythin'," Ryan said. "What have I got to lose?"

"Let's do it, then."

"There's only one problem," Ryan said.

"What's that?" Clint asked.

"What if they get where they're goin' before nightfall?"

Clint looked at Randolph, who shrugged.

Once the sun went down completely they slowed to a walk. The moon was about half-full, which was useful. The worst thing that could happen was that one of the horses could step into a hole and snap a leg. Clint didn't think that would happen to Duke, who was always surefooted. He didn't know about Randolph's horse, though, so he followed directly behind Ryan so that Randolph could follow directly behind him.

Ryan's mare was an enigma. The animal always looked as if she were on her last legs, and yet she kept going and going—sort of like her owner.

They rode most of the night without coming upon the two braves, and Randolph started to worry out loud.

"What if they didn't camp—"

"Shh," Ryan said quickly. He rode back to Randolph before he continued. "If they're ahead of us they'll hear your voice loud and clear," he whispered.

"What if they didn't stop?" Randolph whispered back.

"They did."

"How do you know?"

"I can smell a fire, and it's not far ahead of us," the old man said.

"Will we reach them before daylight?" Clint asked.

"I think so," Ryan said, "but we'll have to do the same thing they did to sneak up on us."

"Go on foot?"

Ryan nodded.

"Now?" Randolph asked.

"No," Ryan said, "not yet. We still have a little ways to go. I'll let you know when, but once we get that close we can't talk, understand?"

Both Clint and Randolph nodded, and Ryan started off again with them following.

Clint was starting to be pretty amazed by the old man. He'd had no idea of Ryan's talents when he first hired him. The man was probably the best tracker he'd ever encountered, and that was certainly an extra bonus. All he'd expected of Ryan was to show them to the tree.

Abruptly, Ryan stopped and turned in his saddle. By the light of the moon they saw him wave for them to dismount. The ground around them was flat, so all they could do was ground their horses' reins and hope they wouldn't walk off. Somehow, Clint thought that only Randolph's mount was in danger of doing so.

"How far ahead?" Randolph asked.

"A hundred yards or so."

"I don't see their fire," Randolph said.

"Wouldn't we see their fire?"

"There's probably a rise between us and them," Ryan said.

"Then how do you know—"

"I told you," Ryan said, "I can smell it."

"How are we going to do this?" Randolph asked.

"Got an idea, Virgil?" Clint asked.

The old man grinned and said, "Yup."

It wasn't much of an idea, Clint admitted later, but then the simplest things often worked the best.

They split up and approached the camp—once they spotted it—from different directions. If it appeared that the two Indians had heard one of them, they agreed to rush the camp.

Fortunately, one of the Indians apparently had a bottle of whiskey, and while the two braves were busily working on it, the three of them were able to creep almost into their laps.

At the last minute the two braves heard Randolph approaching, but as they stood and reached for their weapons Clint fired one shot at their feet and they froze. Ryan and Randolph joined him in camp.

The eyes of both Indians widened as they obviously recognized Ryan by his metal nose.

"How drunk are they?" Clint asked.

Ryan picked the whiskey bottle up off the ground and showed it to Clint. It was less than half full.

"You speak English," Clint said to one of them. It was the man who had stood on his wrist. "I know you do."

The man didn't say a word. Clint looked at the other one, who stared back. He had no idea if this man spoke English, but he knew the other one did, so he concentrated on him.

"Do you ride with Pima Joe?"

The man didn't answer.

"You want me to ask him?" Ryan asked.

"No," Clint said, "he speaks English."

Ryan stepped back and took a swig from the Indian's whiskey bottle.

"Scott," Clint said to Randolph, "this is your show. You want to kill one of them so the other one talks?"

Randolph frowned, then caught on.

"Sure, Clint, it would be my pleasure."

Clint pointed to the first man.

"This one speaks English, so kill the other one."

"Right."

Before Randolph could even pull his gun, the second Indian shouted, "Wait!"

"Silence!" the first one said.

"It is not you who they are going to kill," replied his companion. He looked at Clint and said, "I speak English . . . good English."

"I guess so," Clint said. "Now the question is, will you answer our questions? Because if you won't, there's still no reason to keep you alive."

He matched stares with the Indian for a few moments, and then the brave looked down at the ground.

"Ask your questions," he said.

THIRTY-FIVE

They decided to rest awhile at the Indians' camp, so while Ryan tied both Indians up, Clint and Randolph went for the horses.

When they returned Clint found Ryan working on the whiskey bottle.

"Virgil," he said.

Ryan peered up at him.

"Don't worry," Ryan said. "I ain't a drunk. I just need it for my old bones."

"Yeah," Clint said, "sure. Make some coffee and we'll all have some for our bones."

"Yeah," Ryan said, "okay."

The one Indian had been very cooperative. They now had the location of Pima Joe's camp, and an idea of how many men he had. With only three of them against over a dozen braves, the odds were not good. Still, Pima Joe did not know they were

coming. Also, he didn't know anyone other than
Virgil Ryan.

They sat around the fire and tossed around ideas
for a plan. Clint was the one who came up with
the only viable idea.

"Like I said earlier," he said, "Scott and I will
just ride in. There's no reason for them to think
we're after them."

"You're white men," Ryan said. "What makes
you think they won't just kill you?"

"They live by raiding, right?"

"Right."

Clint shrugged.

"We'll just have to come up with an idea for a
raid that will keep them interested."

"And us alive," Randolph added.

"Long enough to find your wife."

"If she's there."

"If she's there we'll have to find a way for you
to talk to her."

"And if she's not?" Ryan asked.

"Then we get out."

"And what am I supposed to be doing all this
time?" the old man asked.

"The Indian said that the camp is surrounded
by high ground."

"And they have guards."

Clint eyed Ryan.

"How hard would it be for you to avoid their
guards, Virgil?"

"Not hard."

"Then you find a likely place and position yourself with a rifle."

"Right."

"Make sure you keep that nose covered," Clint said. "We don't want the sun reflecting off of it."

"I know how to lay low."

Clint remembered their first meeting and said, "Yeah, I know you do."

Clint picked up the bottle of whiskey and poured the remainder out evenly into each of their coffee cups. "Here's to a successful plan."

They all drank.

"When do we put this into effect?" Randolph asked.

"We'll head out at midday," Clint said. "According to the Indian, we should reach the camp just before dark."

"And that will let me get into position in the dark," Ryan said.

"Right."

Ryan ran his finger around the edge of his cup and then licked it off. "Sounds like a good plan to me."

"Sure," Randolph said, "you don't have to ride into a camp full of cutthroats."

"Cutnoses."

"What?" Randolph asked.

Ryan pointed to his nose and said, "They're cutnoses."

Randolph stared at the old man for a few moments, and then suddenly he was laughing uncontrollably, joined by Clint.

"Was it that funny?" Ryan asked.

THIRTY-SIX

When it was time to go, they had to decide what to do with the two Indians.

"Kill 'em," Ryan said.

Clint wasn't sure he wanted to do that. He wasn't sure he could do that, not in cold blood.

"We can't afford for them to go walkin' into camp while you're there," Ryan pointed out. "The only thing to do is kill them."

Clint looked at Randolph.

"I agree."

"Okay," Clint said, "then you do it."

Randolph hesitated.

"They took your wife, Mr. Randolph," Ryan said.

"They didn't take her," Clint said, "Pima Joe did."

"They coulda been with him," Ryan said.

"And maybe not."

"What do you think we should do with them?" Ryan asked Clint.

"Leave them tied up, I guess," Clint said, "and leave them here."

"If we do that," Ryan said, "one of two things happens. One, they get loose and get to the camp. In that case, you're both dead."

"And second?" Randolph asked.

"They die from the heat, or from starvation, or from thirst," Ryan said. "It's better for them, and us, if we kill them now."

Unfortunately, Clint thought, it made sense.

"I'll do it if you want," Ryan said. "I ain't squeamish."

"Clint?" Randolph asked.

Clint looked at the two Indians, who were bound hand and foot and gagged. Killing a man in that position, even an Indian who probably would have killed them the day before, did not sit well with him.

"I'll do one, Virgil," Randolph said, "and you do the other. After all, it's my wife we're looking for." He looked at Clint and added, "There's no point in you having to do this."

Clint wanted to argue, but what would his argument have been? Both Ryan and Randolph had some reason to kill these men, and he had none. So why not let them do it? And if they didn't do it, did it make any sense to even go ahead with the plan if these men could show up in the middle of it?

"Do it," Clint said darkly. "Go ahead and do it."

Ryan looked at Randolph and said, "Knives. It's quieter and neater."

Clint wanted to turn away, but he didn't. Ryan got behind one of the Indians and, with a happy cackle, slit the man's throat from ear to ear.

Randolph got behind the other one, but instead of slitting his throat he drove the knife into the man's back and twisted it until he was dead.

Clint felt sick.

"We better get going," Ryan said, "but first we should kill their horses."

"Kill their horses?" Randolph asked. "Why?"

"So they don't show up back in camp."

Clint wanted to protest, but if he had stood by and watched two men be killed, how could he justify arguing about two horses?

"I won't kill the horses," Randolph said, surprising Clint and Ryan.

"Why not?" Ryan asked. "We just killed two men."

"They deserved to die," Randolph said, and then added, "maybe. But not the horses."

"What do you suggest we do with them, then?" Ryan asked.

"Run them off in the opposite direction."

Ryan shook his head.

"Eventually they'll turn around and head right back to camp."

"Or to water," Randolph said. "If they head for water it will be a while before they get back to camp."

"Look, Mr. Randolph—" Ryan started.

"And even if they go back to camp, they could have simply got away from their riders,"

Randolph went on, not giving Ryan a chance to talk. "There's no reason to think that Pima Joe and his men will suspect us of anything."

Ryan looked at Clint.

"Talk to him."

"It's his show, Virgil."

Ryan rubbed a hand over his face and then shrugged helplessly.

"Okay," he said, "set 'em free."

Randolph set the two ponies free without their blankets. This way if they found their way back to camp it would look like they could have got away in the night.

The two ponies took off running away from the camp without any hesitation.

"They won't stop running for a while," Randolph said.

"For both your sakes," Ryan said, "I hope so."

They saddled up and rode away, leaving the bodies of the two Indians, still bound and gagged, lying next to the cold fire.

Once again Virgil Ryan had Clint looking at him in a whole new light.

THIRTY-SEVEN

It was almost dark when Ryan handed Clint the reins to his horse and said, "Wait here."

"Why?" Randolph asked, but the old man was already moving away on foot.

"He knows what he's doing," Clint said.

"Doesn't that surprise you?" Randolph asked. "I mean, when you first met him didn't you think . . ."

"Yeah, I did," Clint said, "I didn't think much of him, but now nothing he does would surprise me—except why he chooses to live the way he does."

"Maybe," Randolph said, touching his own, "it's the nose."

Clint thought about that. People probably pointed and stared when Ryan walked down the street, so it would make sense, then, that he'd choose to live in some isolation, going into town only when he had to.

"I'm sure with his talents he could get a decent job somewhere," Randolph went on, then added, "if it wasn't for his nose ..."

Clint was about to answer when Ryan reappeared.

"They're there," he said, "up ahead."

"How far?"

"A couple of hundred yards," Ryan said. "They found a perfect place to camp. There's a depression up ahead that's almost like a valley, with higher ground all around it. There are tipis all around, and one wooden shack."

"And Pima Joe?" Randolph asked.

"I didn't see him, but I know he prefers a wooden shack to a tipi."

"What else does he prefer?" Clint asked. "I'd like to know as much about him as I can before we go in."

"Actually," Ryan said, "he would have preferred being a white man. He wears a holster like a white man and he prefers white women."

"With red hair?" Randolph asked.

"Red ... or blond. Indians don't see much of either," Ryan pointed out. "Your wife must be some woman if she's been with Pima Joe for ten years."

"She was ... very courageous."

"Did you see any sign of her?" Clint asked.

"No," Ryan said, "not in camp."

"How many men?"

"Looks like all of them, except for the ones we took care of."

"About a dozen."

"Right."

"How are we going to handle a dozen men?" Randolph asked.

"Virgil," Clint said, "how good a shot are you?"

"I hit what I aim at," the old man said.

"How many men are on watch?"

"Just one."

"Then we'll start with him. . . ."

They decided that Virgil Ryan should be the one to sneak up on the lookout and take him out.

Ryan went off, and Clint and Randolph gave him what they considered enough time to get into position.

"What if he gets taken, instead of the other way around?" Randolph asked.

"That," Clint said, "would throw a hitch into our plan, wouldn't it?"

"So we're just going to assume that he's in position?" Randolph asked.

"That won't be the only chance we take, Scott," Clint said, "just the first."

THIRTY-EIGHT

When Pima Joe returned to his shack, he found the woman he called Fire Hair fully dressed. In fact, she was wearing a faded blue dress, the clothing of a white woman.

"What is this?" he asked.

She turned in surprise; she clearly hadn't heard him enter.

"I just wanted to try it on," she said, holding her hands across her breasts.

"Where did it come from?"

"I've had it . . . all these years," she said, looking down at the floor.

He stared at her, then asked, "Was that what you were wearing when . . ."

"Yes," she said, "it was."

He crossed the room quickly, batted her hands away, gripped the dress at the neckline, and then ripped it from her. She was left with only a few wisps of cloth hanging from her, while he held most of the dress in his hand. Two of his fingernails had left scratches on her left breast, which she ignored.

Now that she stood naked before him, she did not affect any modesty. Her hands were down at her sides.

"Do you have any other such clothes?" he demanded.

"No."

"Never do I want to see you wearing something like this," he said. "Do you understand?"

"Yes."

She was breathing heavily, and he watched with growing lust as her breasts rose and fell. He saw that her nipples were hard, and took that to mean she was aroused. In point of fact she was frightened.

He tossed the dress away, reached out, and gripped her breasts in his hands. He squeezed hard.

"You're hurting me," she said, flinching.

"Do not move away!" he commanded, and squeezed her even harder.

In spite of the pain, she stood her ground.

He slid his hands beneath her breasts and used his thumbs to rub her nipples.

"Lie down," he said.

She obeyed, lying on her back on the blanket. She watched as he stripped, revealing a huge, pulsing erection. She knew by the look in his eyes that he was so excited that he was going to hurt her. He got like this sometimes, and all she could do was lie back and endure it. Pima Joe did not understand at all that some women would respond more to gentleness than to brutality.

He got on his knees over her, spread her legs, and ruthlessly drove his erection into her. She bit her lip so she would not cry out.

He began to slam into her, harder and harder, and she wrapped her arms around him and raked his back. It was the way she exhibited her pain, but he took it for pleasure and rode her even harder.

She forced herself to moan out loud; he enjoyed it when she made noise, and once had beaten her for not doing so. Her cries excited Pima Joe even more.

She stared up at the ceiling as he drove into her and suddenly, unbidden again, the face of her white husband sprang into her mind. She gasped in surprise, but Pima Joe simply took it as another cry of pleasure.

She closed her eyes and tried to push the memory away. She could not understand why suddenly it was stronger than it had been in years.

"Okay," Clint said, "it's time."

"Are you sure?"

"No," Clint said to Randolph, "I'm not, but I guess we'll find out soon enough, huh?"

Clint started Duke forward and Randolph followed, shaking his head.

From his position above the camp, Virgil Ryan watched Clint Adams and Scott Randolph ride into Pima Joe's camp. He looked down at the body of the man whose throat he had cut and began to softly cackle. He knew that Clint Adams was going to be the man to help him get his vengeance.

Soon, Pima Joe, very soon.

THIRTY-NINE

As Clint and Randolph rode into the center of camp, a group of men gathered there to meet them. Over by the tipis the women huddled together, and Clint saw one white woman and thought that she fit the description of Francis Healy's wife.

They rode up to the men, who waited in a semicircle, and when they reined in their horses the men formed a full circle around them.

They waited.

Pima Joe was standing over his Fire Hair when someone banged on the door of the shack.

"Come."

A brave entered and was caught up short at the sight of his leader standing naked over his white woman, who was also naked. He could not take his eyes from the pale skin of the woman.

"What is it?" Pima Joe demanded.

"Strangers have ridden into camp," the brave said, his eyes still on the woman.

"How many?"

"Two."

Pima Joe reached for his leggings and pulled them on.

"White?"

"Yes."

Pima Joe looked down at the woman and said, "Stay there!"

"Yes," she said, closing her eyes and putting her arm across her breasts to hide them from the other brave.

"Out! Out!" Pima Joe shouted, and pushed the other man out of the shack ahead of him.

Clint saw the two men coming from the shack, one pushing the other. The man doing the pushing was a massively built man wearing a pair of leather leggings and no shirt. His chest was like a slab of stone.

"Take their guns," Pima Joe said as he approached.

Abruptly Clint and Randolph were stripped of their handguns, and their rifles were pulled from their saddles.

The huge Indian stopped in front of them and said, "Give me one reason why I should not have you killed right now."

"Are you Pima Joe?"

"I am."

Clint looked around.

"I would have thought the camp of the great Pima Joe would have been richer, and more festive."

"What?"

"Fine food, even finer women, a house instead of a shack," Clint went on. He looked at the Indian and shook his head. "You cannot be Pima Joe."

"But I am," Pima Joe said, looking confused. "If I am not Pima Joe, then who am I?"

"I don't know, but you don't look like Pima Joe."

Pima Joe stared at the white men and considered having them killed immediately, but he did not want them going to their death doubting who it was who was killing them.

"Bring them," he said.

Clint and Randolph were pulled from their horses and, as they had agreed on earlier, they didn't resist.

Randolph, in the grip of two braves, hoped that Clint knew what he was doing. He'd always thought that he'd either find his wife or die during the attempt, but he didn't want to be the cause of Clint Adams's death.

Pima Joe led the way away from his shack and toward the tipis. As he approached, the women scattered, but he shouted something in his own language and two of the women stayed.

"Here!" Pima Joe said, pointing to the ground by one of the fires.

Clint and Randolph were hustled to that spot.

"Sit," Pima Joe said.

They sat.

The braves fanned out around them, and Pima Joe stood in front of them, his legs spread, his arms folded across his chest.

"Explain," he commanded.

"Explain what?" Clint asked, acting dumb.

"Explain why you say I cannot be Pima Joe."

"Look," Clint said, "I came here to find—"

"Explain," Pima Joe said, "or die."

Clint hesitated and exchanged a glance with Randolph, who appeared calm. Clint figured that Virgil Ryan must be in position by now, or they'd know about him being caught.

He took a deep breath and started.

"Well, I have heard many tales of Pima Joe's raids," Clint said, "and of the great wealth he has stolen."

"This is true," Pima Joe said with pride.

"Where is the wealth?" Clint asked. "I do not see it here in these ragged tipis and one falling down shack. I do not see it in the food."

Pima Joe frowned.

"What else?"

"Your women," Clint said, "are not dressed in finery, and they are ugly."

The Indians around them—the ones who understood English—bristled at having their women called ugly.

"They are not all ugly," Pima Joe said.

"So you say," Clint said, "just as you say you have wealth, when I see none."

"Why did you come here?" Pima Joe asked angrily. "To die?"

"To join you," Clint said, "but now that I see how you live, your women, your men, I do not think I want to."

"I did not ask you to!" Pima Joe said.

"You would have," Clint said, "once we spoke, and once you tested me."

"Tested?"

"Yes," Clint said. He took a deep breath before continuing. "I can outshoot, outfight, and outfuck any man in your camp."

"Out . . . fuck?" Pima Joe repeated, frowning.

"Lie with a woman better than any man in camp," Clint explained.

His words angered the men around him, who probably would have killed him if not for Pima Joe.

"And all of this you are prepared to prove?" Pima Joe asked.

"Yes," Clint said, "that is, I was, but now that I see your camp—"

"Wait," Pima Joe said.

The big Indian obviously wanted to think about what he'd heard. Clint looked at Randolph and saw a thin sheen of sweat on the man's face. He knew that his face looked the same. He hoped that Pima Joe would attribute it to the heat.

"I will show you my wealth," Pima Joe said, "and my women, and then we will test you."

"What if I don't want to be tested?"

"You have no choice," Pima Joe said. "You will be tested—both of you."

"Not him," Clint said.

"Why not?"

"He is with me," Clint said, "but he cannot do the things I do."

"Why not?"

Clint assumed a haughty look and said, "Because no man can."

"Pima Joe can!" someone said, and the other men shouted their agreement.

"We will see," Pima Joe said, raising his arms to quiet them. He looked at Clint and said, "You will be tested, and if you fail even one test, you will die . . . both of you."

Pima Joe switched his gaze to Randolph, who shrugged and said, "I wouldn't have it any other way."

He was surprised he got the words out without croaking from his dry throat.

FORTY

Pima Joe told Clint that they would begin the next morning.

"Why not now?" Clint asked.

"It is getting dark," Pima Joe said. "I cannot show you our riches in the dark. We must have the sunlight."

Clint didn't like this. What if someone went up to where Ryan was to relieve the guard there? They could only hope that the man Ryan had obviously killed was scheduled to be on watch all night.

"What do we do until then?" Clint asked.

"I will give you a tipi, and you will be fed."

"That's generous of you," Clint said. "I had not heard of Pima Joe's generosity. It is one of the signs of a great leader."

Pima Joe did not reply, but his chest swelled. As

Clint had hoped, the man had an ego and enjoyed having it stroked.

Pima Joe said something in his own language and four Indian braves escorted Clint and Randolph to an empty tipi and pushed them inside.

"This is not working out the way we planned," Randolph said. "We didn't expect to be disarmed."

"We didn't plan on it," Clint said, "but it's really not a surprise."

"So what do we do when the shooting starts?"

"There are plenty of weapons around," Clint said. "We'll just have to grab some."

"What was that stuff about being able to outfuck anybody?"

"Once I realized he had an ego—as we had hoped—I had to throw that in. With men like Pima Joe, sometimes their sexual prowess is the easiest to pick at. Also, I figured it would anger some of the other men. Now they all want to see me proved wrong."

"I know you can shoot," Randolph said, "but can you fight?"

"I can handle myself."

"And can you . . . ?"

Clint smiled and said, "I can handle myself, but I really don't expect it to come to—"

He was interrupted by the arrival of two Indian squaws with bowls of food. Both women were dark-haired, but there the similarity ended. One was young, slender, and pretty while the other was older—possibly in her thirties, although Clint found it hard to tell with Indian women. The older one was not unattractive, but was not as pretty as the other squaw. She was also more sturdily built than the other. They both eyed Clint as they handed the men their bowls of food.

"Thank you," Clint said.

The women stared at him for a few moments, then giggled and hurried out.

"What was that all about, I wonder?" Clint said.

"I think maybe they were taking a look at you."

"For what?"

"Well," Randolph said, "you did say you could outfuck any man in camp. Maybe those are two of the candidates."

"At least they're pretty," Clint said. "I saw some of the women out there who weren't—to say the least."

Randolph stared down at the meat in his bowl.

"I wonder what this is."

"I don't know," Clint said. "Horse, dog . . ."

"Dog?"

Clint tasted it, moved it around his mouth, then nodded and said, "It's dog."

"Dog?" Randolph asked.

"Did you ever think you'd eat snake meat until the first time you did?"

"No."

"But you've eaten it, right?"

"Well, sure," Randolph said, "although it's not high on my list."

"Well, I've had dog before and it's not high on my list, but I'm hungry."

Randolph nibbled at a piece, thought about it, then shrugged and put a bigger piece in his mouth.

"Not bad, huh?" Clint asked.

"Not bad," Randolph said, "and not good, but at least it's edible. Jesus."

"What?"

"I just thought about poor Virgil. What's he going to eat?"

"He's probably got some beef jerky."

"What if they send someone up to relieve the guard that he's, uh, already relieved?"

"We just have to hope they don't."

Randolph fell silent for a few moments, then said, "I'm sorry I got you into this, Clint."

"You didn't," Clint said. "I got myself into it, remember?"

"Well . . . now you have to pass a test when I should probably be the one—"

"It's my idea, right?" Clint asked. "Besides, I can outshoot you."

"And the rest?" Randolph asked, with one of the few smiles Clint had seen on his face.

"We'll have to wait for some other time to find that out."

FORTY-ONE

Clint awoke when somebody entered the tipi. He reached over and nudged Randolph.

The fire they had built in the center of the tipi had been reduced to glowing embers. In the near dark someone threw some more wood on the fire, and it flared up, lighting the inside of the tipi.

"Uh-oh," Randolph said.

Their visitor was one of the women who had brought them their food, the older, more solidly built one.

"It's still dark out," Clint said.

"Almost morning," the woman said slowly.

"Ah," Clint said, "Pima Joe wants to start at first light?"

"Start now," the woman said.

"What?"

She smiled, stood up, and removed her leather dress. She had probably chewed every inch of that leather herself to soften it. As the dress fell to the ground, the fire illuminated her naked body. She had large breasts, very round and firm. Her hips, belly, and thighs were solid and full. Given his choice of women, Clint might have picked the other, but obviously he wasn't to have a choice.

"Start test now," she said, and lay down next to Clint.

"Well," Randolph said, "time for me to leave."

When he got to the tipi flap, though, he was not allowed to leave. There were two braves standing there on guard.

"It looks like I'm not going to be allowed to leave," Randolph said.

"Maybe you're supposed to be a witness," Clint said, slapping the woman's hands away from his clothes.

"Start test now," she said, grinning. Her teeth were not white, but at least they weren't rotten. Luckily, Indian women didn't kiss.

"I'll do that," he said, and started to unbutton his shirt.

Randolph went back to the blanket he was sleeping on and said, "Uh, I'll just turn my back and leave you two lovebirds alone—as much as I can."

"Why, Scott Randolph, you sly dog, you," Clint said, "you do have a sense of humor."

FORTY-TWO

Thankfully, the woman had bathed and was clean. The only smell she emitted was a natural one.

Despite his protests, she helped him remove his clothing, and when he was naked she immediately lay on top of him. Her body was solid and warm, and she was eager.

"Wait," he said, pushing her away, "wait."

"Test now!" she said anxiously.

"Lie back," he said, pushing her down on her back.

Clint was not used to making love to a woman with someone else nearby, but he tried to push Randolph's presence from his mind and concentrate on the woman.

Indian women knew very little about the art of lovemaking. It was Clint's experience that what they knew most was simple penetration without much in the way of foreplay.

He pressed his hand to her belly first and then slid it downward. When he had his hand between her legs he found her moist with anticipation. He kept his eyes on her face, and as he touched her for the first time with his fingers her eyes widened and she caught her breath. He was willing to bet that no one had ever touched her down there like that.

When he inserted a finger she gushed and gasped loudly. She reached down to grab him by the wrist, but she did not pull his hand away. Instead, she pressed it more tightly to her, and even lifted her butt from the ground.

He fondled her for a while, until she was almost delirious with pleasure, and then he crouched over her and put his mouth where his hand had been. He was positive she had never had this done to her before, and when she screamed he knew he was right. He ministered to her orally for a while, her moans and cries loud enough to be heard outside the tipi, and then finally he lifted himself over her and entered her. Immediately, she wrapped her powerful thighs around him and they began to rock together. He was about to explode inside her when suddenly her whole body tensed, and then she screamed and bucked beneath him and screamed again when he exploded. . . .

When two Indian women entered the tipi a short time later, the woman was still lying on the floor, unable to move. Clint and Randolph watched as they wrapped her in a blanket, helped her to her feet, and assisted her out of the tipi, throwing curious and wondering looks Clint's way.

"I'm sure they're surprised she's still alive," Randolph said. "I was here and even I thought you killed her."

"Indian women only have sex one way, most of the time," Clint said. "All I did was show her some things she'd never experienced before."

"Well," Randolph said, "I'd say you passed the first test, wouldn't you?"

FORTY-THREE

They came for Clint and Randolph several hours later, and Virgil Ryan watched from his vantage point as the two men were walked out to the center of the camp. Ryan didn't know exactly what was going on, but even he had been able to hear the screams of the woman in the tipi earlier. He had been tempted during the night to slip down into camp to talk to Clint and Randolph, but had decided against it. It wasn't worth taking the chance of being caught. The next time Pima Joe got ahold of him maybe he'd cut something else off. He decided it was better just to stay where he was and wait for the signal he and Clint had talked about just before they parted company.

Still, it was difficult to watch from where he was, without any idea of what was going on. Also, they were bound to send another man up to relieve

167

the guard he'd killed, which meant he was going to have to kill another man. While that would reduce the odds, it would also increase the chances of his being discovered.

He hoped that whatever Clint was planning down there, he'd get on with it soon.

Clint and Randolph waited for the appearance of Pima Joe, guarded by all of the men in camp.

"They're not taking any chances," Randolph said.

"I guess they all want to see the test."

"You think they'll admit you passed the first one?"

"I doubt it."

"Maybe they'll just kill us and be done with it."

Clint thought that the tone of Randolph's voice might indicate that wouldn't be the worse thing that could happen to him.

"I know what you're thinking," Randolph said, "and you're wrong."

"I am?"

"Even if I wanted to die, I wouldn't want to take you with me."

"Then I guess we'll just have to do what we came here to do."

At that moment the door to the shack opened and Pima Joe came out. Clint was watching the man approach when, behind him, at the window, he thought he saw something. He thought he saw a woman looking out—a woman with red hair.

"Clint . . ." Randolph said.

"I saw. Is it her?"

"I can't tell," Randolph said. "Not from here."

"I hope Ryan is as good a shot as he says he is," Clint said quickly, as Pima Joe reached them.

"You choose," Pima Joe said.

"Choose? Choose what?"

"The man you will fight."

Clint looked around and could see that all of the men were anxious for him to choose them.

"I took one of your tests already," Clint said. "Now I think you should show me something."

"Show you what?"

"Something a real leader would have."

Pima Joe frowned.

"What?"

"A woman."

"We have women."

"No," Clint said, "a leader's woman. A beautiful woman, unlike the other women here."

"Ah," Pima Joe said, nodding as if he understood, "you mean a white woman."

He said something aloud and waved his arm. One of his men came forward, his hand clutching the elbow of the dark-haired white woman they had first seen when they entered camp.

"Here is a white woman."

"Not good enough," Clint said.

"What?"

Clint pointed.

"She has dark skin and black hair, just like an Indian woman," he said. "A leader such as you are would have a special woman, unlike any other woman in camp."

Pima Joe stared at him.

"If you do not," Clint said, his heart pounding, "then kill me now, and I will go to my grave knowing that Pima Joe is not the great leader I have heard about."

Pima Joe continued to stare at him, and Clint could feel the tension in the air. He knew that if he took off his hat and tossed it into the air Virgil Ryan would start shooting. He chose the man he would rush, the man whose weapon he would grab, and hoped that Randolph was doing the same.

"You will wait."

Where else would I go? Clint wondered to himself.

From inside the shack the woman known to Pima Joe as Fire Hair, and to Scott Randolph as his wife Helen, was staring out the window, careful to stay out of sight. She eyed the two white men curiously and found one of them familiar to her. He looked older, but he stood the same, tall and strong.

Suddenly she knew that if this was indeed her white husband, after all these years, she did not want him to see her like this.

Pima Joe walked back to his shack, went inside, and reappeared dragging a woman. It was obvious that she did not want to leave the shack, but she was no match for the strength of Pima Joe. Clint thought that the fact that she was naked might have had something to do with her reluctance.

Pima Joe dragged her to where Clint and Randolph were waiting and then dumped her unceremoniously on the ground.

"This is my woman," Pima Joe said, puffing out his chest, "unlike any other woman in camp."

Clint looked at Randolph, who was staring down at the woman. She kept her face averted, her eyes downcast, not looking at the two white men.

"This," Pima Joe said, "is Fire Hair."

Suddenly the woman looked up at Clint and Randolph, and Clint heard the other man take a sharp breath, and then whisper a name.

"Helen."

FORTY-FOUR

There was an even more tense moment as Clint waited to see if Pima Joe had heard Randolph whisper his wife's name. Apparently he had not, but Clint saw the look of recognition in the woman's eyes and knew that she had.

"Do you see?" Pima Joe demanded.

"Yes," Clint said, "I see."

She was dirty, and her hair was tangled, but Clint knew that at the time of her abduction she must have been a real beauty. Even now, ten years later, cleaned up she would still have been a handsome woman. Sitting there naked on the ground there was something earthy and undeniably sexy about her. Now he understood how her husband could have searched ten years for her. He just hoped Randolph could stay in control a little longer.

"So now you choose," Pima Joe said.

Clint had been in life or death situations before, and this was definitely one. Unarmed and surrounded by at least ten Indians, all of whom would love to kill him, he knew that to have any chance to save his life and the lives of Scott Randolph and his wife there was only one choice possible.

"I choose you," he said to Pima Joe.

Ryan saw the brave in plenty of time. He was definitely coming up to relieve the man he had killed. There was no place for him to hide, however, so he hauled the dead body up into a sitting position and hid behind it.

Sometimes being a smaller man paid off.

"Me?" Pima Joe asked.

"That's right."

Pima Joe gave Clint a pitying look.

"You have chosen certain death."

"Perhaps," Clint said, "and then again perhaps not."

Pima Joe stared at him for a few seconds then nodded and said, "As you wish."

He shouted something and his people, men and women, formed a wider circle.

He grabbed Helen Randolph by the wrist and hauled her to her feet.

"Go back inside!" he ordered.

She stared at him, then looked at Scott Randolph one more time before obeying. Clint saw Randolph watch her as she walked back to the shack—as did every other man out there.

"Easy, Scotty," Clint muttered. "Soon."

"Prepare yourself," Pima Joe said to Clint.

"What weapons?" Clint asked.

Pima Joe smiled, showed Clint his huge hands, and said, "I will kill you with my bare hands, and you will know who the great leader is."

Clint backed away and Randolph went with him.

"You're doing great, Scotty," Clint said, as he rolled up his sleeves.

"It's killing me," Randolph said. "After all these years . . . Clint, we've got to get her out of here."

"We will," Clint assured him.

"How?"

"You know what the signal is," Clint said. "Wait for the right moment."

"When will that be?"

"When everybody's attention is on Pima Joe and me," Clint said.

Clint removed his hat and thought about tossing it in the air to signal Ryan, but it wasn't the right moment. They needed total shock and surprise on their side, and that meant while everyone was watching him and Pima Joe.

"Clint," Randolph said, "he'll kill you."

Clint handed Randolph his hat and said, "Don't let him."

FORTY-FIVE

As Clint moved out to meet Pima Joe, there were a lot of things going through his mind. One, even if they succeeded in rescuing Helen Randolph, they still didn't know if she'd want to go back to her husband.

Two, he had several choices among Pima Joe's men as to who he would rush when the shooting started.

Three, he fervently hoped that Virgil Ryan had run into no trouble, and was indeed waiting patiently—and awake—for the signal to commence firing.

As they reached the center of the circle, Clint drove all those thoughts from his mind because he knew if he didn't concentrate fully on the matter at hand, Pima Joe would probably kill him.

The Indians forming the circle were all shouting, no doubt urging their leader on to crush the impudent white man—especially since this white man had shown one of their women a night unlike any she had ever seen before.

Clint circled Pima Joe, and the big Indian circled him, his arms stretched out from his body. Ryan had told Clint that Pima Joe had in many respects adopted the white man's ways. Clint only hoped that boxing wouldn't turn out to be one of them.

He decided to wait for Pima Joe to come to him, and hoped that the man wouldn't be able to patiently outwait him.

"Are you afraid?" Pima Joe asked.

Clint didn't answer.

"Come, attack me."

Still Clint did not reply.

"Ahhh!" Pima Joe shouted then, and attacked Clint.

Clint timed the big Indian's rush perfectly and sidestepped him, putting his foot out to trip him. Pima Joe went sprawling onto the ground, sending up a great cloud of dust and dirt. Some of the men forming the circle actually started to laugh, then thought better of it.

Pima Joe sat up and turned over and glared at Clint, his pride hurt. Clint thought if he could get the man angry enough, he'd lose his head and leave himself open for some kind of finishing move.

As Pima Joe got to his feet, Clint stepped in quickly and hit the man in the face with two left jabs, then danced back. Pima Joe shook his head, then frowned and put his hand to his nose, which was bleeding. As the brave stared in surprise at the blood on his fingers, Clint stepped in and hit him again with two left jabs, and then a hard right. Although the man's nose bled more heavily, he did not take one backward step. This concerned Clint, because he felt he had hit him with a pretty decent right. The fact that the man just stood there and glared at him did not make him happy.

He braced for Pima Joe to rush again.

Virgil Ryan watched the action and was finally able to figure out what was going on. Pima Joe was testing Clint. Usually when that happened the leader let the white man choose his own opponent. That meant Clint had chosen Pima Joe himself. Not smart, if Clint had any intention of actually surviving the confrontation, but very smart if he wanted to attract everyone's attention in camp.

Ryan looked over at the two dead men lying nearby. He'd been worried that someone might come looking for the man who had been relieved, but now he knew why that hadn't happened. No one in camp wanted to miss the action.

Ryan had also seen the red-haired woman, so he assumed that sometime during the fight between Clint and Pima Joe it was Scott Randolph who was going to give the signal to start shooting. That was why Clint had given him his hat.

Ryan sighted down the barrel of his rifle. Pima Joe was the biggest man in camp, and so was the best target. Clint Adams might actually be in the way, though, so Ryan had second and third targets picked out.

He kept the rifle trained on the camp and waited.

Randolph watched the fight intently, so much so that he almost forgot that he had a signal to give. Clint was doing very well up till now, but Randolph could see that Pima Joe was getting angry. Anger could work for you in a fight—it sometimes made you almost impervious to pain—but sometimes it worked against you—it made you careless.

He also watched the other men in camp and saw that they—as well as the women—all had their eyes on the two combatants.

He had almost decided that it was time to give the signal when Pima Joe suddenly charged Clint and caught him in a bear hug.

It was definitely time!

He took Clint's hat and tossed it high into the air.

Clint tried to sidestep Pima Joe's charge again, but the man had learned his lesson and adjusted. He felt those powerful arms close around him, pinning his arms to his sides, and knew that if Randolph didn't give the signal now, he was in trouble.

Suddenly, there was a shot.

FORTY-SIX

A man screamed.

Pima Joe opened his arms and whirled around in surprise.

Clint fell to the ground but immediately kicked out, catching the big man on the kneecap. Pima Joe shouted in pain, but Clint did not wait to see if he went down. He immediately charged one of the other men. Caught by surprise, the man went down easily. Clint struck him in the face with his elbow and pulled his rifle away from him. Even as he turned he was already firing.

He could hear other shots being fired and assumed they were coming from Virgil Ryan's rifle and whatever weapon Scott Randolph had been able to grab.

From one knee Clint fired, levered another round, and then fired again as quickly as he could. By the time the men in camp recovered from their surprise, their force had been cut in half.

Clint saw across the way that Randolph had a rifle and, standing over a fallen man, was also firing.

Suddenly the remaining men turned and ran instead of trying to return the fire. The women were running, too, back to their tipis, hoping that while they hid inside, their men would be able to save them.

It was not to be.

The shooting was over almost as suddenly as it had begun, and Clint and Randolph looked around, rifles ready, to see if anyone was going to put up any resistance.

They walked toward each other and met over the fallen body of Pima Joe. The big Indian had a hole in his back, obviously put there by Virgil Ryan.

"I guess he was right," Clint said.

"Who?"

"Virgil."

"About what?"

Clint indicated Pima Joe and said, "He said he could hit what he aimed at."

"Lucky for us."

They both realized that it was the presence of Virgil Ryan—a man they had both originally thought of as just a crazy old coot with no nose—that had enabled them to pull this whole thing off.

Clint nodded, and then they both turned as they heard someone running toward them. It was

Virgil Ryan, running and cackling at the same time.

"I got 'im, I got 'im," he shouted as he reached them. "I couldn't get 'im with the first shot because you was in the way, Clint, but once he dropped you I drilled him dead center." The small man started kicking the dead body, shouting, "Cut off my nose, will ya? I'll show ya!"

Randolph pulled Clint away and asked, "Should we stop him?"

"No," Clint said, "let him go."

They continued to look around, but the camp seemed deserted. The remaining men had fled, and the women were hiding in their tipis.

Then they both turned their attention to the shack.

"I think it's time, Scott," Clint said, "time to put this quest to rest."

"I know," Randolph answered, but he didn't move. Instead he looked at Clint and swallowed. "What if she doesn't want to come with me? What if she hates me for killing Pima Joe? Or for letting her get captured in the first place?"

"I don't know, Scott," Clint said, gripping the man's shoulder, "but there's only one way you're going to find out, isn't there?"

Randolph nodded his head, then turned and started walking toward the shack.

Even Virgil Ryan stopped kicking Pima Joe's dead body long enough to observe what was going to happen.

As they both looked on, the door opened, and the red-haired woman, Helen Randolph, wearing a buckskin dress, stepped out.

Watch for

THE EMPTY GUN

161st novel in the exciting GUNSMITH series
from Jove

Coming in May!

WESTERNS!

NO OBLIGATION

Mail the coupon below

To start your subscription and receive 2 FREE WESTERNS, fill out the coupon below and mail it today. We'll send your first shipment which includes 2 FREE BOOKS as soon as we receive it.

J. R. ROBERTS

THE
GUNSMITH